# *Stealing Home*

## A *Complicated* Story

# By Wendi Zwaduk

Stealing Home
Copyright © 2015, Wendi Zwaduk
Edited by Michele Paulin and CJ Slate
Ebook Cover Art by Kris Norris
Print Cover by WZDesigns

Published by Megan Slayer Publications
2018
Print Cover Art by WZDesigns


Warning: All rights reserved. The unauthorized reproduction or distribution of this copyrighted work is illegal. Criminal copyright infringement, including infringement without monetary gain, is investigated by the FBI and is punishable by up to 5 years in federal prison and a fine of $250,000.

Electronic Release: March 2015
Print Release Summer 2018

This is a work of fiction. Names, characters, places and occurrences are a product of the author's imagination. Any resemblance to actual persons, living or dead, places or occurrences, is purely coincidental.

# CONTENTS

*Chapter One*     pg   1
*Chapter Two*     pg   13
*Chapter Three*     pg   27
*Chapter Four*     pg   39
*Chapter Five*     pg   53
*Chapter Six*     pg   67
*Chapter Seven*     pg   81
*Chapter Eight*     pg   94
*Chapter Nine*     pg   107
*Chapter Ten*     pg   119
*Chapter Eleven*     pg   132
*Chapter Twelve*     pg   147
*Chapter Thirteen*     pg   161
*Chapter Fourteen*     pg   176
*Chapter Fifteen*     pg   189

*Epilogue*     pg   201

*About Author*     pg   205

*Previews*     pg   206

# DEDICATION

*To JPZ …you know how I feel. Love you.*

*MP…thanks for believing in me and my work.*

# *Chapter One*

*Oh, my God. They're having sex...again.*

Bliss yanked the covers over her head and tried to block out the sounds of her roommate, Jessa, and Jessa's boyfriend making love. Again. Every night, Bliss had to listen to them going at it in the bed below hers. Even after she'd said something, they hadn't stop. Truth be told, she'd grown accustomed to the moans and creaking, but still. No one should have to listen to this for forty-three nights in a row.

She held as still as possible on the top bunk of the bunk beds. At twenty-one, she hadn't had much experience with boys or sex. She squeezed her eyes shut. Guys were a mystery. They never said what they meant, expected things she couldn't do and wanted more than anyone should give. She imagined her only boyfriend,

Ben. They'd dated for the last month of high school. She'd been too involved in academics and art to have time for boys, but he'd gotten under her skin.

Her head ached. Thinking about him wasn't fun. After a month, he'd wanted to screw around. When she'd said no, he'd broken things off and called her a whore. How could she be a whore if they'd never had sex?

Bliss moved the covers and glanced over at her cell phone. Jessa and her boyfriend had been going at it for more than fifteen minutes. Shouldn't they be done by now? She'd heard her friends laugh about how guys never lasted more than a few minutes. Not this guy. Or was Jessa faking? Who knew? Bliss didn't truly want the answer.

Her thoughts turned to Ben again. They'd only gone out for a month, but she'd liked him. He'd been the lone guy to show interest in her. What was it about her that repulsed boys? She didn't know.

"Oh my God. Evan. Evan," Jessa cried. The creaking stopped, only to be replaced by panting and groaning. "Wow."

Bliss rolled her eyes. Wow? She sighed. Maybe, they'd finally realize she was still up there.

"Isn't your roommate here again?" Evan asked. The sheets rustled, and the creaking started back up. "Bliss?"

"Right here." *As always.* "Don't mind me." Bliss rolled onto her side and faced the wall.

"Don't worry about her. She's got a thing for voyeurism," Jessa snapped. "Bliss, go back to bed."

*Christ.* Bliss yanked the covers over her head again and wished the world—especially Jessa and Evan would melt away. If she had to go through another night with them screwing beneath her, she'd scream.

"Jess, we could go to my room," Evan said.

"I refuse to get naked around your gross roommate, Rick," Jessa replied. "Either stay tonight or go. I don't care." She harrumphed, and the bed creaked again. "Personally, I'd rather have a room to myself. Roommates suck."

*Make it go away. Make it go away,* Bliss thought. She'd been berated by Jessa plenty of times, but never with someone else listening. She didn't want to consider what Evan might think when he heard Jessa's snobby words.

"I've got a test in chem tomorrow. I need to get going." Evan's footsteps thumped on the floor. "Bye, Bliss. Sorry." He clunked around the room, probably getting dressed, then the door clicked. Light filtered into the room for a moment then another click.

Bliss thought about rolling over and replying to Evan before he left, but didn't. Jessa wouldn't be pleased, and now, Bliss would have to deal with her roommate's snarky attitude.

Still, hearing him say he was sorry roiled in her stomach. She didn't want his pity. She wanted him and Jessa to have sex somewhere else.

"You made him go," Jessa snapped. She kicked the mattress from the underside, booting Bliss in the hip. "You're a horrible roommate."

*Look who's talking.* Bliss settled into an uneasy sleep. Dreams of Ben, Evan and Jessa filled her head. They moaned, groaned and screwed their way across campus, all while yelling at her. *This is what you won't do. Voyeur. You're too prissy. Lighten up and grow up.*

She woke up five hours later, no more refreshed than when she'd gone to sleep. Getting through her Art History and Greek Lit classes would be killer. She dressed and grabbed her stuff for the bathroom. The faster she got out of the dorm, the better.

"Trying to sneak out." Jessa rested her hands on her hips. "You moaned all night."

"Sorry." The tips of her ears burned. Damn it. The dreams must've been louder than just in her head. "I didn't mean to." When the hell had Jessa even gotten up? She usually slept like a log and way past her alarms.

"Thinking about Evan, weren't you?" Jessa blocked Bliss' route from the room. "He's so hot." She folded her arms, bunching her breasts. Her sleep shirt pulled against her chest, accentuating her already buxom figure. "Are you turned on by him?"

"I don't really like him." Bliss skirted Jessa and headed for the relative safety of the communal bathroom. She'd never actually admitted her feelings toward Evan. Until the night before, she hadn't really cared for him either way.

The pity in his voice had irked her. He'd felt sorry for her having to listen. The nerve! He easily could've left before they had sex, or they could have had sex in his room. Bliss didn't care if his roommate was *gross*. Listening to Evan and Jessa fucking in the lower bunk was pretty darn gross.

"What's your problem with him?" Jessa stood at the sink next to her. Her blonde hair bounced when she talked. "If you have a problem with him, then you have one with me. He's going to play professional baseball, you know? Another year at the college level and he'll be ready for the major league draft." She nodded and grinned. "I'm going to be the wife of a pro-athlete."

"Oh for the love of God." Bliss squished toothpaste onto her toothbrush. Wife? Already? They'd only been dating a short time and most of that time had been spent in the sack. Did he even have slots in his schedule to practice and play baseball?

"You're jealous. I can tell." Jessa's smile widened. "Still hate him?"

"I don't care what he does or what you're planning to do. My problem is that I don't want to listen to you have sex, but it's fine. I'll get earplugs or go somewhere else." Maybe, she could hang out with her friend, Kade, for a night or two here and there. He didn't have a boyfriend that she knew of, and he'd always been good to her. Too bad he was gay or she'd have dated him.

"Going somewhere else would be good. I asked for a single this year, but instead, they gave me you." Jessa frowned at herself in the mirror. "God. I feel fat today, and I look like shit. Look at these bags under my eyes." She pinched her apple cheeks and pursed her lips. Even without gloss or other makeup, she looked good enough to go out in public. Bliss had never understood Jessa's belief she was ugly.

From her perky boobs to her teeny waist and the fact she could wear size six jeans with room to spare, she reminded Bliss of models in magazines. Bliss shook her head and brushed her teeth. She'd never look perfect like Jessa. Guys whistled when Jessa went by. If they didn't, Jessa sulked.

Bliss wondered what it would feel like to be desired. Probably wonderful.

"I'll have to work the bronzer really hard today." Jessa tousled her ponytail. "I won't have much time. My English professor had the nerve to schedule a test today. I don't have time for a test."

Bliss spit out the toothpaste. "Do you know what the test is over?"

"A book. Duh." Jessa crinkled her nose. "It's always over books."

"Which one?" Bliss rinsed then wiped her mouth. She put the toothbrush away. When she glanced at herself in the mirror, she didn't groan. For not getting much sleep, she didn't look half bad. Her hair needed brushing and a little makeup wouldn't hurt, but all in all not bad. Walking around campus had helped trim a few pounds from her frame. Unlike Jessa who'd probably be a perpetual size six, Bliss worked hard to stay in a size ten.

*You've inherited the Haas bone structure,* her mother claimed. *Great if you want to be a fullback, but not so great if you want to look dainty.*

She ran the brush through her hair. She wasn't built to play football, but she'd never be a petite girl. Oh well.

"Did you hear me?" Jessa slapped Bliss' arm. "I said it's some Old English book."

"*Beowulf?*" Bliss secured her dark hair with an elastic band then slipped the flyaway hairs behind her ear. "I read that last semester. You needed to pay attention. Good luck." She breezed past Jessa and headed back to their dorm room. She switched out of her sleep shirt and into a pair of jeans, a bra and fresh T-shirt.

She slipped a sweatshirt over her head then flipped her hair out from under the collar.

Jessa stomped back into the dorm room. "Look, I know you're pissed about our living arrangement. I'm not wild about it, either. I said single, and they put me in this crappy double with you. No, I haven't read *Beowulf*, and no, I didn't pay attention. I'm not here just to get my degree."

"I can tell." Bliss scooped her books into her backpack. "I hope you and Evan will be very happy."

"We will once you leave." Jessa grasped the door handle. "This is my room, too. I can have all the sex I want, and there's nothing you can do about it. Got me? Nothing."

"I could go to the resident assistant," Bliss muttered. But that wouldn't work because Jessa had become best buddies with the RA. No matter what Bliss said, the RA would take Jessa's side. Money tended to talk louder than reason sometimes. Besides, she and Jessa were both juniors. They should've been able to sort out their problems on their own.

"You do and you'll be sorry," Jessa snapped. "So don't even. Evan and I are going to be happy, and if that means fucking our brains out until he realizes he loves me, then fine."

"That's…sad." Bliss stared at her. "You value yourself so little that you're willing to force him into something he may or may not want just so you can, what? Marry money? Are you sure it's worth the trouble? What if you're both miserable?"

"We will never be miserable. You'll never understand."

A knock on the door interrupted the rest of her tirade. Jessa opened it.

"You're early," she said. "But I'm glad you're here."

Bliss glanced in the mirror. In the reflection, she saw Jessa and Evan in the open doorway.

"Can we talk in the hallway?" Evan didn't look at Jessa or Bliss. "It's important."

"See?" Jessa clapped her hands. "Everything will be perfect." She clicked the door shut, effectively leaving Bliss in the room.

Bliss checked her watch. She had fifteen minutes before she had to leave. Great. Let them talk out whatever was bothering Evan. She didn't need to go anywhere.

"What do you mean?" Jessa shrieked.

Bliss froze. Jessa was prone to dramatics, but then she was a drama major. Still, she actually sounded upset. Bliss grabbed her backpack and eased closer to the door.

"That was shitty of you. Come on. She's got a right to the room, as well. We can be in my room or my car," Evan said. "You're being a bitch."

"I am not." Jessa's voice dropped to a dull roar. "Call me that one more time, and I'll break your arms. My dad's rich. I can have someone break your arms for me."

"God." Evan sighed. "This is why things aren't working out. Look, I've got to go. I'm late for class."

"So you're what? Dumping me?" Jessa's voice rose in pitch. "Evan?"

"It's not like you're magically going to be nicer to your roommate, so yeah, I'm dumping you. Call me an asshole, but I can't take your drama. Be the sweet girl I met, and maybe things might work out."

Bliss jumped back from the doorway. Holy crap. She didn't have a whole lot of experience with guys, but she knew enough to recognize when the shit had hit the fan. She'd also have to make herself scarce for a few days until Jessa cooled down.

"I don't believe it." Jessa burst into the dorm room. Tears streaked down her face and splotched on her black T-shirt. "He…dumped me." She turned her attention to Bliss. "It's your fault."

"Whoa." Bliss inched back to the door. "I didn't say a word."

"You knew." Jessa's eyes narrowed, and her lips curled in a sneer. "Don't you dare come back to this room."

"I have to. My stuff is in here." Now, she wasn't so sure any of her things were safe.

"Never come back." Jessa reached for Bliss.

Thankfully, Bliss dodged the shove and ducked into the hallway. She hurried to the stairwell and down the stairs as fast as possible. Hell hath no fury like a Jessa scorned.

* * * *

For the next three days, Bliss spent as much time as she could away from the dorm room. She slept at Kade's apartment or stayed out until she knew Jessa would be asleep. Not the best plan for getting any kind of rest or getting her homework completed, but she managed.

Thursday, she headed back to the dorm room. They'd have to sort out their differences sooner or later. She knocked on the door.

"Jessa?" Bliss twisted the knob and crept into the room. "Are you here?"

Jessa lay curled up on the bed with her back to Bliss. "Why did you come back?"

"I had to. I need my books." Bliss dug through the milk crate for the art history book. She should've taken the course earlier in her college career, but she'd been unable to work in the extra class.

Jessa rolled over. Her makeup had smeared over her cheeks, and her hair stuck out in odd tangles.

"Have you slept in a while?" Bliss brushed a lock of Jessa's hair from her face. "He really screwed you over, didn't he?"

"I thought I loved him." A tear streaked down Jessa's cheek. "He was supposed to be the one."

"I'm sorry." She knelt beside the bed and petted Jessa's hair. "I understand. Things don't always work out." She bit back her shock. In the three months they'd shared the dorm room, she and Jessa hadn't talked about anything other than surface topics. Deep conversations weren't Jessa's thing, as she'd said. The change of pace was quite nice.

"Let's not talk about him, okay?" Jessa wiped her face. "I'm done." She sat up then flipped her hair over her shoulder. "I need to call Daddy to come get me. There are parties at home. I don't want to miss them."

"Okay. Cool." So much for having an endearing moment. Bliss scooted out of the way. "What parties? Someone's birthday?"

"Oh, I don't know. I'll find one." Jessa shrugged. She picked up the phone then ducked into the hallway.

Bliss sighed. At least, Jessa wasn't upset. Maybe, they'd get past the incident with Evan and be able to finish out the year without another issue. Probably not.

## *Chapter Two*

Bliss walked across campus to the art building. The situation with Jessa didn't sit well with her, but dwelling on it wouldn't change anything. She trudged down the two steps to the foyer then yanked the door. In less than a week, she'd have a test. The professor expected the students to know more than a hundred slides and at least twenty terms. She knew the artwork and the vocabulary, but after the week she'd had, she wasn't sure she'd be able to concentrate to study.

She headed into the main auditorium ten minutes before class. Most of the seats in the upper section of the room were already filled. She didn't mind. She preferred to sit closer to the front in order to see the slides better. She placed her bag on a second seat then turned around.

"Bliss?" Evan grinned at her. He held his backpack strap. "Never thought I'd see you here. How have you been?"

She froze. Unlike most of the students, she didn't really hang out with the others in the class. "I'm good. I haven't seen you at the dorm. I know you and Jessa split, but I figured she'd con you into coming back."

"She's like that." He shrugged and sat on the other side of her bag. "Has she talked about me?"

"Well…" She opened her notebook and pulled out one of her pens. "She's upset. You embarrassed her. Was it of her own doing? A little, but I think she really did like you. She said something about getting married and being the wife of a ballplayer."

"Good God." He laughed. "She has no idea."

"What do you mean? I thought you were on the baseball team."

"I am, but I have no desire to go pro." Evan opened his own notebook. "I got the scholarship to play and I love the sport, but I don't want to play in the major leagues. I want to coach."

"Oh."

"I'm probably good enough to go pro, but I don't have the heart for it. I want to play for the love of the game, not because I've got a contract to fulfill." He shrugged. "My major is physical education. One more year and I'll be able to work in the schools and start coaching."

"I see."

"Aren't you an ed major, too?"

"Art education."

"Thought I saw you in the education building." Evan sighed. "So the reason I'm over here, versus sitting in the back, is that I need you."

"Excuse me?" She'd never thought of him in a romantic light, but then she'd never seen him anywhere besides the dorm room. Even then, she hadn't really looked at him. Being so close to him without Jessa in the middle, she could see why Jessa had been attracted to him. He'd brushed his dark blond hair off his forehead. When he smiled, his blue eyes twinkled. He didn't look as if he'd shaved in a day or so. She wanted to slide her fingertips over the prickly little hairs on his cheeks. His cologne wrapped around her. For a moment, he overwhelmed her. What would it feel like to be the woman in his arms?

"Bliss?" Evan waved his hand in front of her face. "Hello? Earth to Bliss."

Oh crap. She'd spent too much time thinking about what could happen, all while knowing she and Evan weren't going to hook up.

"I'm sorry. I'm here." The tips of her ears burned. "What did you need?"

He smiled again. "I need you to help me pass this class. I'm failing miserably. Help?"

"I'm not dating you," she blurted. She wasn't sure why she'd said that since she'd just imagined him cuddling her.

"Um...okay. I wasn't asking." He chuckled, and the light in his eyes glittered.

"I thought it was a bad pickup line." Not a good cover, but she'd sort of explained her goofy answer.

"It was cheesy and something I probably would've said to get a girl, so you got me." He clasped his chest. "Guilty as charged."

"You're silly."

"I try." He grasped her hand. "But seriously, I need help. I'll get kicked off the baseball team if I don't pull this grade up."

"It's that bad? One grade will get you kicked off?"

"I'm one D away from losing my spot." He let go of her hand. "We have to maintain a three-point-five to stay on the team. Coach insists we have a real degree and keep our academics up. He's right. We can't play ball forever. Gotta have a back-up plan."

She gripped her pen and considered her options. If she worked with him to pass the tests, she'd have to spend time with him. They'd have to keep out of Jessa's way. Did she want to bring on the wrath of Jessa if she found out? Did she even want to be around Evan, the man she'd nicknamed the horny toad?

"Well?" Evan asked. "I'm begging."

"Fine. I'll help you." She nodded. "I've got an hour after class. We can go to the student center. Second floor has tables where we can study."

"And stay hidden." He nodded slowly. "I get you. Don't get Jessa involved. Smart."

"Well, duh. If she finds out, she'll be pissed. Number one, she'll want to rip out my hair for helping you. She wants you to die. Number two, she'll gouge out my eyes for what she'll see as double-crossing her for even being seen with you. Number three, she'll accuse me of trying to sleep with you because I was supposedly so turned on from listening to you and her have sex."

"Ouch. She's that pissed?" Evan frowned. "We dated a month."

"You were the Energizer Bunnies of sex," Bliss spat.

"You *did* name us that." Evan laughed again. "I thought I heard you say that, but I decided I was losing it." He shook his head. "It's true. We worked well in bed, but once we had to talk to each other, everything fell apart."

"Since all you did was have sex, I'm not surprised."

"The name is deserved. And now, we're done. Why? Because I hated how she treated you. Everyone in the damn dorm heard her. When I said something to her on the sly, she flipped out again. Amy had to come down and split us up. Do you know how embarrassing that is? The fucking RA getting involved. Why she didn't write us up is beyond me."

"Jessa probably conned her into letting it slide. She does that." Bliss pointed to the front of the room. "If you've got an hour after this is over, I can help. But he's about to start."

"Cool." Evan opened his textbook on the extra tablet desk then smoothed his notebook paper. "We're up to the Baroque period. If it ain't Baroque, don't fix it."

"Shh." She stifled a giggle behind her hand. His joke was horrible and one she'd heard plenty of times, but he'd made her laugh. She shouldn't give him credence, but oh well.

The professor talked about the works of Vermeer. "Look at the play of light and dark in this painting."

"What painting?" Evan murmured.

Bliss reached across him and turned the pages of his book until she found the right work. She pointed to the painting.

"Oh. Thanks," he whispered.

The lecture progressed with mentions about Vermeer's life then the professor moved on to Rembrandt. Each time Evan grunted or whispered to her, she pointed out the specific reference. Forty-five minutes later, the professor left the front of the room and the lights brightened.

"Wow. I'm missing so much. He doesn't put half that info on the slides." Evan flopped the book shut. "No wonder I had no idea what he was talking about."

"Once you learn Professor Marin's style, it's a lot easier." She slid her notebook into her backpack. "Ready?"

"I am."

Bliss maneuvered through the throng of students exiting the building. Once they were outside, the bright sunshine warmed her cheeks. She breathed in the crisp air. "No snow yet."

"It's only the third week of November." Evan fell into step beside her. "Can't snow until December first."

"I don't mind winter, but I cherish each day that's not yucky. I hate walking across campus in snow."

"It's one day closer to baseball season opening. We do conditioning all fall and winter. Once it's March, the games start." Evan bumped her shoulder. "Have you ever gone to one of the games?"

"I haven't. I'm never sure where you play. They switched the fields when they put in the new rec center." She reached for the door.

"Allow me." Evan grabbed the handle and held the door for her. "I have manners. Might not seem that way, but I do."

"Thank you." She eased past him but brushed his chest with her shoulder. The touch shouldn't have tingled all the way down her arm, but it did. She held her breath until she got away. He wasn't going to affect her. No way. She'd seen Jessa fall all over him. She would *not* do the same.

He didn't say anything as they went up the main stairs to the second floor. She stopped at one of the study tables tucked behind a wall.

"This should be good." She dropped her bag on one of the chairs. "Now, where are you lost?"

"Since the last test. I bombed it." Evan sat opposite her. "The different kinds of churches confused me."

"I know. If you don't pay attention to the nuances, you can get really mixed up." She opened her textbook. "Saint Chapelle features lots of blues and gold. Tons of stained glass. They wanted lots of ornamentation. Notre Dame has the three deep portals and has the gargoyles."

"Like the movie." Evan turned the book around. "What about this one?"

"Those are depressed arches with carved ornamentation at King's College Chapel."

"I'm so lost."

"We'll get you there." She flipped to the section on Rembrandt. "We have to know his work. You can do that." For the next hour, she pointed to the different paintings and churches. Little by little, he picked up on the visual cues.

"Cool. I know my Rembrandt from my Vermeer." He winked. "This morning, I wouldn't have known who either guy was." Evan stood. "I have to lift, so I'll see you on Monday?"

"Sure. We'll plan on another study session then. Yes?"

"You bet." He smiled then hefted his backpack onto his back. He waved and walked away.

Bliss blew out a long breath. He shouldn't have taken so much out of her just by studying, but she understood his intensity. He needed to learn the material to stay on the baseball team. The more concentration he put in now, the better off he'd be in the long run. She tossed her things into her backpack then left the library.

She hurried across the courtyard in front of the student center. She glanced over at the new recreational center. Evan was supposed to be there — or at least going there. A visual of him in nothing but his running shorts and jogging shoes came to mind. She'd never actually seen him without his shirt off, but she knew her male anatomy. Would he be smooth or have hair on his chest? Did he have tattoos? She stopped in front of the applied science building. She'd never be able to sit through the basic science class without thinking about Evan, but they were study buddies—nothing more.

She snagged one of the seats near the back of the small auditorium. Although she tried to pay attention, Evan never strayed far from her mind. God, she was lovesick, and the love was so unrequited. Maybe, that was her lot in life—to love but not be loved in return. Love... Good Lord. She barely knew him. Love did *not* happen that fast and certainly not to her.

Bliss jotted down the notes and added the test date to her calendar. Before long, she'd be able to go back to the dorm room and veg out for a while. If Jessa was already gone, even better. No drama.

She stopped at the cafeteria on the way back to her room. The boxed dinner of a cheeseburger and fries wasn't ideal, but at least, it was hot. At the top of the stairs, she paused. Unlike most Friday nights, the common area was full of students. She eased into the large space and stayed on the fringes of the room. The others chatted and pointed toward her hallway, but no one seemed to notice her.

"What's going on?" she asked Aiden, a guy from her Aesthetics class. "Someone died? Or is getting kicked out?'

Aiden snorted. "Jessa's having one of her epic meltdowns." He glanced over his shoulder. "You'd better hide. She's pissed at you."

"For what?" Jessa scarfed down her fries. "What did I do now?"

"She says she saw you with her ex." He shrugged. "She's got so many exes it's hard to know which one you could've been seen with or even why it's a problem. I mean, who cares?"

"She does." Bliss polished off her hamburger. She'd be better off if she kept out of Jessa's sight. Damn. So much for going back and hanging out in her room.

"Thanks for the heads up," Bliss said and patted Aiden's shoulder. "I'm out of here."

"Smart." He smiled then returned to his chemistry book.

She ducked from the room and back into the stairwell. The main floor common area would have to do for now. There she could see Jessa coming and had a better chance of hiding. She shouldn't have to hide, but then she also shouldn't have had to deal with the hysterical dramatics of Jessa, either.

Two hours later, she'd finished all her homework and read the two chapters needed for Monday's classes. She'd even read half of the romance novel she'd secreted into her backpack. Her mother hated when she read the books, calling them "wastes of paper and time". Oh well. The heroine usually got the man of her dreams and the guy always seemed to be dashing, despite his initial coarseness. She wanted to meet a guy like that—someone she could start off hating then fall madly in love with. But life wasn't a fairytale or a romance novel.

She folded her arms and rested her chin on her forearms. Was it safe to head back upstairs? Probably. Bliss packed her things then made the trek back up the four flights of stairs. In the fourth floor common area, the crowd had dispersed.

Bliss sighed with relief—until she rounded the corner to her hallway. A stack of boxes littered the main path.

"What the...?" she mumbled. She hurried to her room. All five boxes had her name emblazoned on them in black marker.

"Finally decided to come upstairs." Jessa stood in the doorway to the dorm room. "Scared of me?"

"I'm a little scared of your mood swings." Bliss clutched her bag. "You're upset with me about Evan?"

"Duh." Jessa rolled her eyes. "I thought we were cool."

"We are." Or so, she'd thought, too.

"Yeah. We're not." Jessa snapped her fingers. "Amy, she's back."

Bliss shook her head. "What's going on here?"

"Well." Amy, the resident assistant, handed her a piece of paper. "Sometimes, we have roommate issues that can't be solved by moving one of the parties. In others, we can. You're being moved once I have a new room assignment. Sounds like it might be a new dorm assignment, since I don't have any rooms on my floor and the others are full. Sucks but then you should've been a better roommate."

"How was I the bad one?" Bliss leaned against the boxes of her belongings. "Because I asked them not to fuck when I was in the room in the top bunk? Because I asked nicely for them to undress in the dark? Or does this have to do with Evan asking me to help him pass a class?"

"All three," Jessa snapped. "I thought about what we talked about. I don't have to be nice to you. You ruined my life."

Amy's dark hair bobbed as she nodded. "You're permitted to enter the room with me until all of your things are removed. I'll have the new assignment tomorrow. Got somewhere you can stay tonight?"

"I need to call Kade."

Bliss wobbled on her feet. Her world had shattered around her. Just when she'd thought things had worked out, Jessa knocked her down. Bliss would need to move the boxes and have Amy watch as she retrieved the rest of her stuff. Thankfully, Jessa had waited until the weekend, but still…being thrown out of the room she'd half paid for… What a load of crap.

# *Chapter Three*

Evan stood at the end of the hallway and watched the scene unfold. From his vantage point, neither Bliss nor Jessa could see him. Fine by him, for now. He couldn't believe Jessa had gone through with having Bliss evicted. He'd met with Bliss one time. How in the hell did Jessa know about the study session?

He gritted his teeth. He needed Bliss if he wanted to pass the Art History class. No way around that. He'd sunk himself by not asking for help earlier.

He debated giving Bliss a hand in moving her stuff, but instead, he hung back. She'd already incurred Jessa's wrath. He didn't need to make things worse. Hooking up with Jessa hadn't been smart. She'd spent more time mad at him than anything. If they hadn't been fucking, they'd been fighting.

A guy hurried up the stairs then rounded the turn, without bothering to look at Evan. Evan had seen the guy before. The moment the man embraced Bliss, Evan's heart squeezed in his chest. She looked awfully cozy with the new guy. Was he her boyfriend? Evan wasn't sure why the jealousy hit or even why it hit so hard. She wasn't his.

"Thanks," Bliss said. She wiped her face then hefted one of the boxes into her arms. "I'll be back for the others in a little bit."

The guy picked up two boxes then followed Bliss down the hallway.

Evan scurried to the window and turned away from them. God, he was a coward. He should've been standing up *to* Jessa and *for* Bliss. No, he was hiding by a window. He'd screwed up so much by *screwing* the wrong woman.

Once Bliss and the mystery guy were down the stairs, he darted into the other hallway to his dorm room.

"You got a phone call." Rick held up a piece of paper. "Interrupted my game."

"Thanks." Of all the people to be paired up with, roommate-wise, he'd gotten a gamer. Evan liked video games and played a few, but not like Rick. The man had circuit boards and game controllers in his blood. When he played well, everything went fine. If he had an off day, everyone had to look out.

"Jessa got persistent. That was actually the fourth call." Rick paused his game. "You're not hitting that any longer, right?"

"I'm not." Evan crawled onto the top bunk of the beds and unfolded the note. He saw the words, but they didn't register in his brain. Instead, he thought about Bliss being in his position.

Listening to Rick grunt and argue with the television wasn't bad, but after a while, he wanted to turn off the game. And those grunts weren't as horrendous as having to listen to him and Jessa screw around. Jessa had refused to be quiet.

"If I brought a girl home, would you stick around while we made out or would you boogie out of here?" Evan folded the paper. "Rick?"

"Honest? I'd watch." Rick stood beside the bed. "You know me and girls. We're oil and water. They want my time, and I'd rather work on my stuff for tech class."

"The gaming is for an actual class?" Evan asked, shocked.

"Yeah." Rick frowned. "I do love the thrill of playing just to cream my opponent, but I'm also developing ways to make the games better and more responsive. That's the wave of the future, man. Getting the player more fully into the game."

"Huh." Evan's appreciation for Rick gathered intensity. The guy wasn't simply taking up space in the dorm, as Evan had assumed.

"Does Jessa want to come over here? I heard she's got a psycho hose beast for a roommate."

"Hardly." Evan sat up and folded his legs underneath him. "Bliss isn't as bad as Jessa makes her out to be."

"If you want to screw Jessa here in the room, then do it. I'll check out—unless it's after midnight. I gotta sleep sometime." Rick shrugged. "I do sleep."

"I know. Thanks, but I'm not bringing her home. She's history." Evan massaged his temples. He'd fucked up so bad.

Rick stared at him for a moment. "Did you fuck her with the roommate in the room? Was she a voyeur or were you just a dick?"

"I was a dick."

"Dude." Rick shook his head. "Did you apologize to Bliss?"

"Not yet." He wanted to—right now, in fact—but he didn't know where she was.

"It's your funeral." Rick laughed. "I had two sisters. They were older, so I couldn't go all brother's-gonna-kick-your-ass on their boyfriends, but they taught me to pay attention. Girls like to be treated nice. Apologize. If you want in Bliss's pants, it'll give you a better shot. If not, then you've got a clear conscience."

"Go back to your video games." Evan laughed with Rick. "Or get your own girl problems."

"I will. I've got my eye on a girl in tech. She's a total geek—more than me. She knows her megabytes."

"I'm sure she does." Evan flopped onto the bed. He read the note again. Jessa wanted to talk. He had nothing to say, but if he didn't stand up for himself…

He needed to end the Jessa chapter in his life.

Evan climbed off the bed and pocketed his keys. "I'll be right back." He forced himself down the hallway to Jessa's room. The door was propped open, and music blasted into the hall. "Jessa?"

She bounded to the door. "You came." Her eyes lit up, and she yanked him into the room. "Good. I've been thinking about you all afternoon. This fight we've had is stupid. I don't hate you. I'm not even mad any longer." She slammed the door shut. "All I want is to be with you."

"Whoa." Evan opened the door in case he needed the quick escape. "I'm not here to kiss and make up."

"You're not?" Confusion clouded on her face. "What… What are you here for? Not Bliss."

"No, not Bliss."

She smiled again and batted her eyelashes. "Good. She's history anyway. I caught her stealing from me."

"Jessa, don't lie." He folded his arms. "She didn't take stuff."

"My sweater is missing. She took it." Jessa strode up to him and smoothed her hands along his shoulders. "If you and I tried kissing and making up, I'm sure it would work."

"No." He removed her hands from his chest. "We're done. I saw you get Bliss kicked out of the dorm. I don't know whose ass you kissed to do it, but whatever. It's done. So are we. Stop calling me, and stop harassing Bliss."

"You're seeing her, aren't you?" Jessa narrowed her eyes. "What's she got that I don't?"

"Compassion," Evan replied. "She put up with your shit when she didn't have to. I'm not even sure why she stuck around so long."

"She wanted to see you naked."

"Well, *you're* never going to see that again. I'm done. Goodbye, Jessa." Evan left the room without giving her a chance to argue. He'd had enough with her crap. Time to move on with his life and finish out his college career, sans drama.

* * * *

On Monday, Evan sprinted across campus to the art building. The days of showing up right before class began were over. He had a reason—beyond the class itself—for showing up. Bliss.

He waited on the bench outside the auditorium. Sooner or later, she'd show up. He'd apologize. He'd even worked out exactly what he wanted to say.

Five minutes before the class started, he still didn't see her. Fuck. She wasn't ditching class because of Jessa…nah. That wasn't Bliss' style. She valued her education—or at least, she must have. She sat in the front of the class and took diligent notes.

He headed into the auditorium.

Bliss sat in her usual seat, with her notebook out and her pen ready.

"Hey you." He sat beside her. "I was out there waiting on you."

"I came in through the second-floor doors." She didn't look at him. "You're early."

He gritted his teeth. Shit. She wasn't the rosy, happy girl he'd come to know. "Hey." He wanted to touch her and reassure her but held back. "Jessa was wrong."

"I don't want to talk about it."

"Well, I do. I'm sorry. We were wrong to put you in that position. Jessa's even more wrong to be holding it against you. I screwed up, and I want to make it up to you."

"Don't."

"I'm not taking no for an answer." This time, he ignored his common sense. He placed his hand on hers. "The least I can do I buy you dinner tonight."

"After I help you out." She frowned at him but didn't pull her hand away. "Don't bother."

"I'm going to bother." He finally got a look at her face. Her cheeks were red and puffy. Fuck. "Bliss. I'm sorry. I am. I'll spend the rest of the semester making it up to you—study help or not. I was wrong."

"I got it." She eased her hand from his and put her finger to her lips. "He's going to give us the outline for the test. Pay attention."

Although, Evan wanted to leave the class and forget art, he did as she'd told him. Knowing what they'd be tested on would make the studying easier. In their first session, Bliss had mentioned noting the nuances to the works on the slides. He jotted little reminders with the titles of the paintings. The Rembrandts had bright whites in the eyes and teeth. The Vermeers showed more emotion. Van Dyck painted kings. Sooner or later, Evan would remember everything.

When the class ended, his head hurt. He rubbed his eyes. "I've never had so much information crammed into my brain at one time."

"You'll get used to it." She closed her notebook. "I saw you taking notes and writing down stuff about the paintings. That's smart."

"Thank you." She'd never given him a compliment before. He liked hearing her say nice things. "I had a good teacher."

Bliss rolled her eyes. She tucked her things into her backpack then withdrew a pair of sunglasses. "I'll meet you in the student center in five minutes."

"Who saw us?"

"I don't know." She hefted her pack onto her back. "I don't care."

"I do." He grabbed his bag and hurried to keep up with her. "For being short, you move fast."

"Force of habit. My friends are all tall." She put on the sunglasses then left the building.

"Bliss." He grasped her hand, stopping her. "You don't have to run away from me. I'm an ass, but I won't bite."

"I got kicked out of my dorm room because of you. I had to sleep at my friend's apartment for the last three nights. He got a boyfriend and I'm trying to stay out of their way. Hence, I'm not going back there tonight. On top of all that, I've got a test tomorrow in my Lit class and I can't concentrate. I'm a little pissed."

"You have every right to be." He let go of her. "But you also can't let her win."

"No?" She snorted. "Jessa already did. She got what she wanted."

"I don't think so." He nodded. "Let's go to the student center. I'm getting cold, hungry, and I want to ask some questions about the Vermeers."

"About what? You know those." She kept up beside him. "He has the deep shadows and focused light."

"I know." He held the door for her. "I get him confused with Caravaggio."

"He was influenced by Caravaggio." She eased around him. "Right time period, though."

"See? This is why I need you." He pointed to the food court. "What would you like? I'm buying."

"Evan." She shrank back from him. "You're sorry. I accept the apology."

"Cool, but I'm still hungry. I need carbs before I lift. What would you like? I hate eating alone." He pulled his student ID from his wallet. "Anything you want."

"Fine. I'll take a salad." She shoved her hands into her coat pockets. "Italian dressing."

"That's all?" He stepped up to the pasta counter. "I'll take a bowl of spaghetti, don't scrimp on the sauce and a salad with Italian. Do you want a drink?" he asked over his shoulder.

"A soda is fine," she answered.

"Two sodas." He drummed his card on the counter. Sodas…he hadn't heard anyone call pop by the other name in a long time. He paid for the food and handed her one of the cups.

Bliss kept on the sunglasses as she poured her drink.

"Do what you want, but you're bringing more attention to yourself with those on." He filled his drink. "You wouldn't be the first girl to come in here looking like you've cried, but if someone says something, blame me."

"I will." She eased the glasses off and tucked them into her pocket. "Better?"

"Much." Now, he could see her beautiful eyes. He picked up the tray. "Where would you like to sit?"

"Somewhere secluded."

"I like how you think." He knew what she meant but couldn't help himself. "Privacy is great."

"I'm not coming on to you." She stalked away from him to a table in the corner.

"I know." He trailed after her. "What if I want you to?" He placed the tray on the chipped, laminate table. "You're a pretty girl."

She rolled her eyes. "You want to be with every pretty girl."

"That's not true." A week ago, she'd have been right. After the implosion with Jessa, he'd begun to rethink his situation.

"Thank you for the salad. I'll help you get through the semester, since we've only got a few weeks left, but that's all." She sat on the chair in the corner. "Don't make this into something it's not. You're only seeing me differently because I'm helping you. It's a proximity thing. If we weren't being thrown together, I wouldn't even make it onto your radar."

She'd cut him to the quick and was completely correct. He wouldn't have noticed her without the class or his failure to pass said class. But what if the class and the crap with Jessa was supposed to happen? What if he and Bliss were supposed to go through the trial in order to find each other? It could be a long shot or it could be the shot he needed. He liked that she wasn't automatically drawn to him. He'd never believed in right place and right time—until now.

## Chapter Four

Evan stood outside the art building auditorium and dragged his finger down the grades list. In the last four weeks, he'd studied his ass off. When he wasn't in the gym or in the batting cage, he'd worked with Bliss to ensure he'd pass art history. He couldn't pass until he finished his tests. The first step was the second major exam. He'd passed that with a B. He looked down the list for his last name for the final exam grade.

"Phillips, Phillips," he muttered. Where was his name? He'd turned in the damn test.

"You're right here." Bliss tapped the bottom of the first page. "He cut it up strangely."

He scanned the line she'd pointed to and damn near swallowed his tongue. B+. Holy shit! "I passed and not by the skin of my teeth."

"I know." Bliss softly punched his arm. "You can master those slides when you want to."

"I did." He tipped back his head and laughed. "I passed the class."

"Looks like."

"I passed." He threw his arms around Bliss and hugged her tight. The euphoria of the moment swept over him. He'd done what he thought was impossible—because of her. He kept her in his embrace and stared at her. Bliss had been his savior.

"What?"

"I'm happy." And she felt so good in his arms. Too good. This wasn't the attraction of having to be together. He liked her. Evan stared into her eyes, losing himself for a moment in the deep blue. He leaned forward. The need to kiss her was too great. He nipped her bottom lip and bit back a moan. She tasted like heaven. Everything within him tingled.

Bliss tugged out of his arms and turned away. She wiped her mouth with the back of her hand. "Why... Why did you do that?"

"What? I'm happy. I wanted to kiss you." He shrugged. "You liked it."

Her eyes widened, and she backed up. She shook her head.

"What did I do? I thought we had a connection." He didn't understand. When they'd gone to breakfast the day before, he'd felt the sparks. "We talked to Kade like we've been together forever. We put Kade's mind at ease. Us. Because we were together."

Without saying anything else, she scurried out of the building.

"I will never understand women," he said to no one in particular. He thought he'd done a good thing. He'd enjoyed the kiss. He'd gone along with her to breakfast to thank her for helping him and to spend time with her outside of the classroom and study sessions. He'd liked those moments together. Now, he wasn't sure what the hell was going on. She'd claimed she had a lead on a place to stay, but…

Evan threaded his hands into his hair then sighed. He returned to the dorm. Rick lay sprawled out on the bed.

"Hey." Rick propped himself up on his elbows. "I need the room for a few hours tonight. I got a date."

"Oh?" Evan switched the books out of his bag. When classes started up after Christmas, he'd need different books. "When are you heading out for break?"

"I'm sticking around. I got a job at the tech lab. A bunch of the foreign students won't be going home, and they'll want to use the computers. I can fix the glitches and bugs that will no doubt happen."

"Cool. When's your girl coming over?" Evan picked up his gear bag. "Meaning, when do I need to get out of here?"

"Fifteen minutes. It's fine. I think Kris and Bliss are friends." Rick snorted. "Kris and Bliss. Whatever."

Evan grinned. He'd had a friend in high school named Annie. They'd been inseparable for their entire junior year—until Annie realized there were more guys in the world than just him. She started seeing the captain of the football team, and Evan had disappeared.

"Am I early?" A blonde stood in the doorway. "Hey, Rick."

"Kris." Rick jumped off the bed. "I-I'll be right back." He darted out of the room.

"What's with him?" She stayed in the doorway. "Did I piss him off?"

"Nah. He's nervous. Have a seat. I was just leaving." Evan hefted his gear bag onto his shoulder. "Have a good night."

"See you." Kris waved.

Evan zipped his coat then went to the stairwell. One of the other guys from the floor, Aiden, held the door open.

"Aren't you the one who was porking Jessa?" Aiden asked.

Evan's cheeks burned. "I did."

"You're the reason Bliss left?"

"In a roundabout way." Evan shrugged. "Why? Did she say something?"

"Jessa did. She wants your nuts on a platter." Aiden folded his arms. "Bliss is a nice girl."

"I know." Odd. He hadn't talked to Aiden since their freshman orientation class. What was his deal?

"I wanted to date her, but God, you can't get past Jessa. If you show interest in Bliss, Jessa jumps in." Aiden groaned. "Anyway, if you're seeing Bliss, be nice to her. She's…she's been through enough."

"More than just Hurricane Jessa?" Evan focused on the other guy. "I'm listening." He placed his bag on the floor of the landing.

"She's got a secret or something. Jessa made fun of her at the beginning of the year when we got our room assignments. She said Bliss wouldn't know what a naked man looked like if one flashed her. Said she was right off the farm. I have no idea if she lived on a farm, but I've seen her hesitate around guys. You'll have to ask Bliss for sure, but trust me."

"I will. You don't happen to know where she is, do you? I kissed her in the art building, and she flipped out. She ran away." Evan picked up his bag. "I've got lifting and practice tonight, but I want to talk to her. There's a Christmas party for the athletes tomorrow, and I thought I'd ask her to come along."

"Last I heard, she took her stuff to her friend Kade's but since he's got a boyfriend, she's been sleeping in the common areas. I'm surprised you haven't seen her—or she's gotten good at hiding from the security guards already."

"Wait. She's been sleeping there? *That* was her plan for housing?" Jesus. She'd been sleeping in the common areas? God. He wanted to wring Jessa's neck for being such a bitch. Then he wanted to kick his own ass for being a jerk. Anger flooded him. When he saw Bliss the next time, he'd give her a piece of his mind. Sleeping in the commons…he bit back a growl.

"If it helps, I heard she spent a couple nights at Kade's. They are good friends, but since he's hooked up with someone…you know how that goes." Aiden chuckled. "Wait, no you don't."

"Ass."

"Have you ever met Kade? He's a nice guy." Aiden flipped through a fat notebook. "Kooky film student, but nice."

"One time. She introduced us." Evan shrugged. He hadn't gotten a bead on Kade in the short time they'd talked, but the guy seemed decent.

"I bet she'd want to go with you, though. She seems nice." Aiden opened the door again. "See you."

"Have a good holiday." Evan hurried down the stairs to the ground floor then across campus to the rec center. He spent the next few hours running through his workouts and focusing on the weight reps, rather than the situation with Bliss. The kiss replayed in his mind. She'd blown him away with a kiss. He'd never felt that way before, and she didn't want anything to do with him. Where had he screwed up? Because he'd kissed her?

She was his friend, sure, but he'd come to like her. He wanted to spend time with her without the books in the way. He'd have to worry about her later and hope Aidan would come through for him.

\* \* \* \*

The next evening, Evan checked his appearance in the rearview mirror once more. He wanted to look his best in case he ran into Bliss. She had no reason to go to the party, beyond seeing him, but he still hoped she'd show. He'd driven to the Sports Medicine building with the intention of driving back home to Cleveland at the end of the night—unless he ran into her. He'd gone to the commons the night before hoping to find her, but she hadn't shown up. He hoped she'd spent the night at Kris' or Kade's. Anywhere but the commons. Maybe, Aiden had gotten the message through and she'd be at the party.

Worth a shot. Evan climbed out of his beat-up car and locked the vehicle. In the reception room, a large Christmas tree glittered. A disco ball sent rainbows around the room and crepe paper had been draped over the I-beams. Music blasted and most of the guys from the baseball team stood together in the corner.

Evan spotted Kris, Rick's date from the night before, hanging out with the other members of the swim team. When Bliss turned, Evan saw her. She rubbed her arms and smiled at one of the guys beside her.

Run over to her? Play it cool? He wasn't sure. She didn't look upset, but then he'd had a hard time reading her. The dress she wore accentuated her curves, and the black material emphasized the paleness of her skin. She'd curled her hair and every time she blushed, the ruddy color stood out. He wanted to wrap her in his embrace, and never let go.

Bliss shrugged away from the guy talking. He put his arm around her shoulders and said something else. Her brow knotted, and she didn't laugh with the group. She eased away from him and disappeared into the throng of people mingling on the makeshift dance floor.

Damn it. He picked up a glass of soda. He wanted to talk to her, not make small talk with the baseball team.

Jeremy, the first baseman, strolled up to Evan. "Did you see the girl who came with Kris Newton? God. She's goofy."

"Goofy?" Evan rolled his eyes. "Where'd you get that from?"

"She can't dance, won't try to dance with anyone and is so shy. She's not even cute." Jeremy laughed. "She and Kris must be good friends. Kris usually holds court with the swim team crowd, but even they aren't hanging around."

"That's mean," Evan snapped. He left his drink on the table. Time to seek out Bliss. She'd looked out of place beside Kris. They might be friends, but Bliss seemed fearful of the noise and bustle in the room.

"Can I rescue you?" Evan touched her elbow. "It's noisy."

Bliss jerked. Her eyes widened. She reminded him of a scared rabbit. "I'm a little overwhelmed." Her hands shook. "I was told you wanted me to attend. I couldn't get in without Kris. This is too loud."

"It is." He offered his hand. "Loud and obnoxious is more my style—but not yours."

"You love this, don't you?" She grasped his fingers. "You feel at home."

"I didn't, but I do now." He eased her to his side. "Why don't we talk a walk over to the courtyard. They decorated the trees and flowers for Christmas. I hear it's pretty with all the twinkly lights."

She hesitated. "I don't know."

"It's quieter." He smiled. "I promise to be a gentleman."

Bliss sighed. "All right." She kept beside him as he walked out of the main space.

Evan steered her to the building's courtyard. The space, filled with various plants and trees, was meant to encourage the students and to provide a welcoming place to study. With the LED lights draped from the small fruit trees and fake snow surrounding the plants, the space looked festive. The play of light and shadow set a certain mood, especially after hours of activity in the building.

He glanced over at Bliss. A smile curled on her lips.

"What's on your mind?" Evan slowed to a leisurely pace. "You ran away from me yesterday."

"I've got lots on my mind." She sighed. "I've got a couple of finals coming up, I don't have a place to stay and I refuse to take incompletes because of my living arrangements. Does that work for you?"

"Stay with me." He'd been rash, but the answer would work. "I'm on the fourth floor, and I've got room. Rick's trying to get a single."

"I can't. You know they won't allow co-ed rooms. Just co-ed buildings." She stopped. "Besides, I can't."

"Why? I don't have a disease." Evan faced her. "I'm housebroken."

"I just... I can't." She closed her eyes.

"Bliss, talk to me. I'm not going to bite you or flip out." Evan clasped both her hands and kissed her knuckles. "I'm pushing too hard, but I like you. I'm screwing everything up by coming on strong, but I don't know how to be anything else. Come here." He led her to one of the benches and sat her on his lap. "Talk to me."

Bliss opened her eyes. "I'm... I don't have a lot of experience with guys." She tensed on his thighs. "I've only dated once, and it was a disaster." She covered her face with her hands.

"Okay." Evan rubbed her back. "Who cares? Some people don't date much."

"I'm a virgin," she said around her hands.

"Cool." He respected her conviction. He'd lost his virginity the night he turned eighteen. At the time, he'd thought he was doing the right thing. Looking back, he hadn't meant much to the girl he'd slept with.

"Cool?" She moved her hands and stared at him. "You sound like I'm a prize to be destroyed. You want to be the guy who can claim he's taken my virginity." She scooted off his lap. "I don't play that way."

"Wait. Bliss." He jumped from his seat. "Stop." He grasped her hand again, keeping her from leaving the courtyard. "Listen. Do I want to date you? Yes. Sleep with you? Eventually. I'm attracted to you and want to see where things can go. Am I going to push you? No."

"Evan." The muscle in her jaw tensed.

He navigated through the courtyard to the gazebo set up in the middle of the area. "Sometimes, a good thing is staring right back at you."

"You're a good thing for me?" she blurted. "You screwed my roommate while I tried to sleep on the bunk above. That's terrible."

"Yes. That was tacky. In hindsight, I shouldn't have done it. But I got to meet you. Without Jessa, I wouldn't be in this moment with you." He curled his fingers under her chin. God, she had soft skin. "I haven't tried to get into your pants. That's gotta count for something."

"True." She balled her fists on his chest. "It's hard for me to trust people."

"I understand." He tipped her gaze so he could look into her eyes. "This is me being completely honest. I like you. I want to help you, and if it means I get to know you even better while you're staying with me, then great. I'll crash on the floor and you get my bed."

"What about Rick?"

"He's moving out after break." Evan's heart beat faster. A few more nudges and he'd convince her. He felt the tension between them going away. He swept his thumb across her cheek. The scent of her perfume wrapped around him. He wanted to kiss her everywhere.

"Evan." Her brow furrowed again. A tear slipped down her cheek.

He eased one arm around her and held her close. Her breath warmed his skin. As much as he longed to kiss away the tear, he didn't. "I'll be in a double occupancy as a single. There will be plenty of room. Stay with me."

"But Jessa—"

"Forget her. She doesn't control me, and she shouldn't have power over you. I'll protect you and give you space. I won't put the moves on you, unless that's what you want."

"What about a trial period?" She clutched the front of his shirt.

"Starting once we get back from break." He wanted her in his arms that night, but he'd been honest when he'd said he wouldn't push her.

Bliss picked at one of the buttons on his dress shirt. Enough with Jessa and the mistakes of his past. Evan covered her mouth with his. When she whimpered, he held her tighter. He'd forgotten how good it felt to kiss—not to screw like rabbits or to go through the motions, but to really kiss. He sucked on her tongue, learning her, and she flattened her hands on his chest. Did she have to leave that night?

Bliss broke free first but stayed in his arms. She rested her forehead against his. "I'm not going home for break."

"Why?" He cupped her cheeks in both hands. "Everyone goes home for break."

"Not me." She half-smiled. "I would if I was wanted, but I'm not. Mom ran off to California, and Dad remarried a woman who hates me. He'd probably like me to come home, but Meredith… It's a complicated story and one I don't like to talk about."

"Then you'll stay with me. No one should be alone over the holidays. Come on." He slipped her hand into his. He'd make things better for her, no matter what. "We'll make it into an adventure."

"Cool," she whispered. "Very cool."

# *Chapter Five*

Bliss sat next to Evan and listened to him sing along with the radio. She'd always wanted to sing, but she didn't have the voice for most songs. She stared out the window and watched the scenery fly by. Part of her couldn't believe her luck. She, Bliss McMahon, had a guy friend who wasn't gay and who was interested in her. He was handsome and kind. She never wanted the moments with Evan to end.

Then there was the rest of her. The part with her crappy self-esteem. She didn't want to sound whiny, but why was he wasting time on her? When would he change his mind and decide she wasn't good enough? Better yet, when would he start laughing at her like everyone else?

"You're quiet." Evan reached across the center console and held her hand. "Is my singing that bad?"

"Nah. You're good." She turned her attention from the blurry scenery to him. In the dim light of the dashboard, he looked even more handsome. Roguish would be the word she'd use. He reminded her of one of her romance novel heroes.

"Both my parents still live in the same house. Still married. Twenty-seven years together. My oldest sister lives in Washington with her husband and little boy. They come back to Ohio in the summer because she hates snow. My other sister moved down by Cincinnati. She was dating a guy named Roland. Last I knew, they were still together." Evan laughed. "Then there's me. I'm the baby."

"Did they dote on you?"

"No. They locked me in the closet, left me in the backseat and generally ignored me once I lost my cuteness." He laughed again. "Then they both realized there were boys in the world and used me to talk to them. I've played ball since I was five. If they came to the games or practices, they realized they could bump into the guys their ages who played, too. That's how Alicia met Carson."

"That's nice." She rubbed the back of his hand with her thumb. He kept finding ways to both impress her and to make her jealous.

"What about you? Your mom moved to California?"

"She wanted to find herself back where she grew up." Bliss sagged against the seat. "Makes sense, now, my name. Mom wanted to be different, and she was. Nothing went quite according to plan. She wasn't the settling down type. Even when I was little, she talked about moving on."

"You mean forward?"

"No, I mean on. She'd had her kid and was done with the mommy thing. Now, she needed to find her center and simplify her life." Bliss looked at Evan. He wasn't laughing or even smiling. "She left, and Dad moved on the best way he knew how. He married his high-school sweetheart, Jan. She started out nice enough, but once the reality set in that I wasn't going anywhere, she turned bitter. Then she had Avery, and I ceased to exist. No pictures, no phone calls…just nothing."

"That's horrible."

"That's life." She'd never shared that part of her life with anyone. Opening up to Evan was surprisingly simple but scary. He hadn't laughed, true, but people could be funny. One moment, they empathized, and the next, they insulted. She didn't want to be the butt of a joke because of things she couldn't control.

"I don't understand how anyone could be that way, but then, I've got it easy, I guess. My parents never let us forget how much they cared about us. I might not be the professional ballplayer Dad wanted, but I know he loves me."

Parents who loved their children. What a concept. She hadn't heard from her mother in more years than she could count and only received a birthday card from her father. He didn't call or check on her. Maybe, she was jealous of her baby sister. Avery got all the attention while she got none. At least, the baby would know she was loved. Bliss bit back her upset. Did she really need the attention of her father? She'd gotten along just fine at college without it. Yes, she kept to herself and made few friends, but other than the loneliness, she was pretty good.

"Your name is fine, and it's pretty. It suits you." Evan kissed her knuckles. "Well, you're welcome in our home and speaking of…I give you the Phillips' homestead." He stopped the car. "I've got the room above the garage. Dad wanted the basement, and Mom didn't want to move my stuff out, so I ended up in the bonus room." He switched off the headlights. "Mom and Dad were going to a Christmas party, so we've got the house for a few hours. My promise is good. No pressure. I've even got bunk beds in my old room."

Bliss climbed out of the car. Before she could retrieve her bag from the backseat, Evan grabbed the bag.

"Mom raised me to be a gentleman. I might be a sweaty ballplayer and somewhat of a player when it comes to women, but I have manners." He offered his hand. "This way." She allowed him to escort her into the house. He paused in the kitchen. "Wait here. I'll take these upstairs then give you the tour."

"Thanks," she murmured. Bliss glanced around the expansive kitchen. She'd never seen so many pots and pans in her life. She trailed her fingers over the tile on the island. Her stepmother would probably give her right arm to have a gigantic kitchen like this one. A photograph caught her attention. When she inspected the image closer, she recognized Evan in his baseball uniform.

"That's me during senior year. Mom had my baseball card blown up. She liked the picture." Evan shrugged. "I thought they all looked the same." He pointed to the hallway. "Here is the peanut gallery. That's my folks, Barbara and Gene. My sister, Alicia, with Carson and Gage. He's already five. It's nuts how time flies. This is Aren. She's the one dating Roland. She's also not a kid person."

Bliss touched the frame around Evan's senior photograph. His sisters were so pretty — all blonde hair and big smiles. They reminded her of the All-American girl types. She'd be willing to bet they were tall, too. She looked at Evan's image again. He hadn't changed much. A few more freckles stood out, and his tan wasn't as dark, but he was still the handsome man from the picture. Good thing they weren't at her father's house. She refused to let anyone ever see her senior photograph.

"The living room is this way, and you've seen the kitchen. Mom insisted on making it bigger. She loves to cook." Evan held her hand. "Dad's den is off this way, and the bedrooms are all upstairs." He tugged her up to the second floor. "There's a bathroom here, and then, there's one off the bonus room, too." He stopped at one of the doors. "Ready?"

"To see your place? Sure."

"You're being guarded again." He didn't open the door. "Tell me."

Looking at the photographs reminded her of all the reasons she wasn't good enough for a guy like Evan. She'd never be pretty enough or thin like his sisters. She laced her fingers together. She had to tell him the truth, but she didn't really want to.

"Hey. I said I won't bite." He tipped his head to look into her eyes. "Please?"

"It's nothing."

"I doubt that." Evan leaned against the door. "You've been quiet since we left the party, but even more so once you saw the wall of shame downstairs."

"You mean wall of fame."

"No, shame. I had horrible hair in high school. Perpetual hat head." When she laughed, he finally smiled. "See? No one is perfect. Why don't you think you're pretty?"

He'd sliced her to the marrow. "I'm short, chunky, and I can be too loud."

"So? You're beautiful, and any guy who can't see that is blind." Evan tugged her into his arms. "I mean that. They were nuts to pass you by. I was nuts."

"You *are* nuts."

He shrugged. "That or I've been pegged in the head by one too many fastballs. But I'm not blind. I see the pretty girl who hasn't been given the best chance in life making the best of what she's got. It's very sexy."

"Don't do this." She pushed away from him. Tears threatened behind her eyes. Damn it. She wasn't going to cry. No. She needed space, but she refused to crumble.

"Don't do what?" Evan allowed her freedom. "Don't be honest?"

"Don't get my hopes up." She blew out a long breath and turned on her heel. Coming home with him had been a ridiculous idea. She didn't belong there. Maybe, she'd listened to her stepmother, Jan's, needling or focused on Ben's mean comments, but she should've stayed at the college.

Evan pinched the bridge of his nose and sighed. "I'm not trying to inflate your ego. A true friend doesn't mince words. Come here." He gathered her back into his arms and gazed into her eyes. "I apologize for the guys before me who were dicks, and I promise to prove them all wrong."

"Sure."

"You'll see." Evan opened the door to his room. "My bed is yours." He waved to a queen-sized bed. "I'll take the bunk bed. Want to watch a movie or are you tired?"

"A movie is fine." She sighed. He moved so fast and kept her on her toes. She should be thankful for him. Should appreciate his zeal. He refused to give her time to dwell. Maybe, that's what she needed—a prod to move forward and get beyond the past.

He strolled over to the television and picked up a VHS cassette. "I love this movie. Change while I get it set up."

Bliss crept into the bathroom. She'd expected guy stuff everywhere—like baseball memorabilia or men's toiletry items. Instead, the room seemed bland. Black tiles on the floor and white cupboards. The walls blended into the cabinetry and shower stall. The room definitely needed personality.

She shrugged out of her coat then pulled on the zipper at her side. The tab refused to move. She yanked and tugged, but with no results. Crap. She needed help.

Bliss walked back into the main room. "Evan?"

He turned around. He'd opened the front of his shirt, giving her a tantalizing glimpse at the muscle and power in his chest. He reminded her of a model in a magazine.

"I need help." She paused. She'd accused him of using a cheesy come-on line, and here she was using one just about as bad. "The zipper's stuck." She pressed her lips together. One day, she'd learn to stop while she was ahead.

"Come here. Show me where the tab's at."

Bliss crossed the room to him and lifted her right arm.

"My sister's hated this kind. The stupid things always got stuck." He placed one hand on her hip and grasped the zipper pull. "My sisters weren't stupid. The zippers were. Mom complained about them, too. When you find new and inventive ways to be a pest, you learn things." Little by little, he opened the dress. "There you go."

"I'm not helpless," she blurted. Holy Jesus, she needed to stop talking.

"I know." Evan grinned. He opened the cuffs of his shirt then removed the garment. "Let me get you a shirt to sleep in." He tossed the dress shirt onto a hamper. "I've got lots."

*Women's sleep shirts*, she almost said but stopped.

"I got this one when we went to the state championships." He placed a white shirt in her hands. "It was huge on me so it should cover you."

"Thanks." She headed back into the bathroom. The urge to clock him settled in her brain. If the shirt was too big for him, it should cover her? What a turd! But she knew what he meant. The more time they spent together, the better she understood him. He wasn't trying to insult her.

She wriggled out of her dress and draped the cocktail garment over the shower curtain rail. She stripped off her pantyhose and placed her shoes by the door. Instead of removing her bra, she kept the lingerie on and eased into the shirt. Evan hadn't been kidding. She could swim in the garment.

"Everything okay?" he asked from the other side of the door.

"I'm good." Bliss opened the door. "Ready for movie time."

Evan patted the couch. He'd ditched his shirt and switched his trousers for a pair of baggy sleep pants. He'd propped his bare feet on the coffee table. "Get comfy. I've got lots of blankets."

She drank in the scene. He wasn't anything like she'd expected. In many ways, he was almost too good to be true. His muscles twisted and bunched as he moved. The blond hairs between his pecs led down to his bellybutton in a thin trail. The downy hairs glinted in the light. She longed to run her fingers over his abs.

"What?" He grinned and blushed. "Second thoughts? Or are you planning on eating me alive?"

"No…on both accounts." She crossed the room and settled beside him. "I'm thinking this was the best idea." And being beside him gave her the chance to touch him.

God, she was lovesick. Her heart ached. She wanted to be loved. Down to her soul, she wanted someone to crave her. When he palmed her knee, she didn't pull away. She couldn't.

"You're warming up to me finally?" He let go of her long enough to drape a thick, fleece blanket across her legs then his arm around her shoulders. "Nice and toasty."

"Thank you." She rested her head against his chest. He'd been a surprise since the moment she'd decided to open her mind about him. She was in his home, in his arms… The last time she'd trusted a guy, he'd screwed her over. "One question."

"One." Evan squeezed her. "After that, I'll charge you."

"Huh?" She paused. What? The more she thought about what he'd said, she caught on to the joke. "Oh. Duh."

"I have a strange sense of humor. No one really sees it because I don't like to open up enough for them to notice. Now, what was your question?"

"This isn't a porno, is it?" The moment the words popped out of her mouth, she regretted asking. "Sorry." Embarrassment washed over her. Talk about going and blowing the moment.

"Do I look like that kind of guy?" He held up his hand. "Don't answer that. No, this isn't a porno. It's a real Christmas movie. I promise." Evan laughed. "Although it would be funny if it was. I can't remember the last time I watched one."

"I believe you." Bliss tucked her knees to her chest. "I guess I'm showing how naïve I can be. Jessa used to say I was so green. Maybe, she was right."

"Hold up." Evan turned in his seat and met her gaze. "I don't know if you're naïve. I don't think so. Why? You've got a good heart. That's hard to find. As you can tell from the house, my folks have some money. I'm not getting any of it, but girls seem to think I'm made of money. You didn't know about my past or any of that, and you still wanted to hang out with me. That's huge." He smiled. "I trust my heart around you."

Bliss closed her eyes as he kissed her again. For the first time since the explosion with Jessa, she felt safe. The weight she'd carried around melted. No more worrying about where she'd sleep or how she'd get her work done. Being with Evan—even if only in a platonic way with a few kisses sprinkled in for fun—wasn't a guarantee her life would stay better, but she wouldn't change a moment of their time together.

"Should we watch this thing?" Evan asked.

Bliss nodded. Soon, Christmas carols rang out in the room. People in red and white garb danced. She'd seen the movie before, but being with Evan made the experience so much better. She wasn't sure what time the movie finished, but when Evan nudged her, she jerked.

"Wake up." He kissed the top of her head. "Either I'm that boring or we're that tired."

"Was I sleeping?" She sat up. Crap. When had she fallen asleep? She scrubbed her hand over her eyes. "I'm sorry. I don't usually crap out during movies."

"We both took catnaps." Evan rubbed her arm. "It's late. You deserve a good night's sleep after I dragged you halfway across the state."

"Thanks but this was my choice. You didn't force me." She stood and glanced over her shoulder. "You really don't mind me taking the bed?"

"Nah. The bunk bed is actually pretty comfortable. Besides, I insist."

"Then thank you." She'd be more courteous in the morning. She trudged over to the bed and collapsed. His scent permeated the pillows. Almost as good as really sleeping with him. She snuggled in the covers and succumbed to the bone-deep weariness. She'd worry about him and whatever it was bubbling between them tomorrow.

## Chapter Six

Evan stretched out on the couch. He shouldn't be staring at her as she slept, but he couldn't help himself. She looked so peaceful...and sexy. She'd curled her hair for the party and worn makeup. The little duckling had sure made a pretty swan.

He should head over to the bunk beds and sleep, but why? He wasn't tired.

His ears perked, and he sat up. Someone was at the house. Had to be his folks. He'd helped his father put in the security system and knew the siren would go off if someone without a key entered the home.

"Evan?"

*His mom.* He grabbed a T-shirt then hurried downstairs. His mother and father stood in the kitchen.

"Hi, honey." Barbara Phillips dropped her purse on the counter. She eased her pale blonde hair from whatever had been holding it. The curls plopped down past her shoulders. "We didn't expect you home until tomorrow."

"I got in early. The party wasn't happening." He shrugged and glanced down at her black spangly cocktail dress. She hardly looked her fifty-six years. "How about your party? I thought Dad said you'd be at a hotel."

"It was good, but I'm bushed, and the hotel wasn't what we expected. Home and my own bed are much better. See you in the morning." She kissed him on the cheek then strode past him and left him alone with his father. Her perfume lingered in the room. Normally, he felt at home in his parents' house. Anxiety crept into his brain. He'd invited a girl home — not that his folks would care — but he'd done it unannounced. On top of that, his father wasn't talking. Never a good sign when Gene Phillips didn't have anything to say.

Gene leaned against the counter and sighed. He remained quiet for a long moment.

Evan hooked his fingers in the waistband of his sleep pants. He never could read his father's expressions. "Hi, Dad." He wasn't sure what else to say.

"Son." Gene stared at him. "Is she a good girl?"

Evan fought to keep his mouth shut. How did his dad know there was a girl here? He'd been discreet. His anxiety deepened. He'd done his share of stupid things in the past, but with Bliss, he wanted to be a better man. Had he overstepped the boundaries with his parents? He hadn't thought before he'd acted, and he had the feeling his actions were about to crash down on him.

Gene nodded to the steps. "This isn't that Jessa girl, is it?"

"No. She and I are no longer." *And thank the Lord for that.* His patience and self-esteem couldn't have handled much more of her verbal abuse. He had bigger and better things to worry about—like the upcoming baseball season, the new semester and winning Bliss' heart.

"Wonderful. She irritated your mother." Gene picked up a fresh glass from the dish rack and poured water from the tap. "We weren't going to say anything unless you brought her home for Christmas. She wasn't right for you."

Huh. His mom put up with a lot from his girlfriends even if she disliked them all. She'd never said anything, which perplexed him. Now, his father—usually short on explaining—clued him in on so much more.

"So?" Gene sipped the water. "Who is she?"

"Her name is Bliss." Evan put both hands in the air. "It's her real name, and no, she's not a stripper or a waitress at a nudie bar. She's in my Art History class. Smart girl and she helped me pass so I won't get kicked off the baseball team. You'll like her. *Mom* might even like her."

Gene's brows rose. "I see. Well, you know the rules. No sex in the house, and if you get her pregnant, that's on your head. Understood?"

"Completely." Evan nodded as if to punctuate his agreement. He'd been told he looked like his father had back in the day. He hoped when he got older he'd inherit his father's wisdom and patience as well as his looks.

"Have you gotten your schedule? For baseball and next semester?"

"Both, actually. I've got to head back to the campus two days after Christmas for ball practice. The season's starting in February this year. We fly to Florida that first week. Classes start the second week of January. I've got my writing intensive class this year. It's mostly writing papers about the history and philosophy of sports and physical activity. I can do the work, but I may need to beg for cash to add memory to the computer. She's old, but she runs like nobody's business. My field experience is in the fall then student teaching in the spring. I've got the big state tests in March, but I should be good."

"You will be prepared, correct?" His father never minced words. "No more dicking around?

These tests are important. Your college career is important."

"I will." He grasped the edge of the counter and thought about the near future. For the first time since he'd set foot on the campus, he knew where he was going with his college career and what he wanted to accomplish after graduation. "Bliss should have to take the same general tests, so at least, I'll have someone to study with. That'll make things a tad easier."

"Good." Gene placed his glass in the sink. "I don't care how long she stays, but remember those rules."

"I will. Good night, Dad." Evan waited for his father to head upstairs via the main staircase then he went back to his room on the second floor.

Just as he'd left her, Bliss lay curled up on the bed. She'd unballed her fists but hadn't stretched out.

Evan knelt beside the bed and eased a stray lock of her hair behind her ear. He'd been a douche bag in his past. Girls had been disposable, like tissues. He'd taken what he needed and moved on, leaving them upset. Back in high school, he'd played the role of bratty rich kid. Going to college had opened his eyes. The dating, the screwing around had showed him being an entitled shit wouldn't help him in life. God, he'd been horrible.

Then he'd met Bliss. He stroked her hair. She'd been the bright spot. Even if she'd initially hated him, she'd given him a chance. The girls in his past had been nice girls—for the most part, but they weren't her. She'd turned his head after a day of actually getting to know her. They hadn't slept together, and yet, he felt closer to her than his former best friends.

He stared at her sleeping form again. He wanted to make love to her. Not fuck or something meaningless but to actually make love. He craved her and down to his core, he wanted to be the man she needed. Was that crazy? After knowing her for only a few weeks? Probably.

He stood and stretched. Would she get pissed if he crashed beside her? No better way to find out than following through. He rounded the bed and pulled back the covers. Instead of shucking his clothes, he stayed dressed and eased into bed next to her. He rolled onto his side and cuddled up behind her.

Bliss sighed. Instead of curling up tighter, she snuggled into him. Her ass wiggled against his groin. His cock reacted and blood rushed below the elastic of his sleep pants. Shit. He couldn't hide a damn erection. Maybe, if he closed his eyes and focused on sleeping, his problem would take care of itself. The scent of her perfume filled his nose, and her hair tickled his cheeks. Hell, she made behaving so hard.

Evan draped his arm around her waist and forced himself to attempt sleeping. Being with her kicked his senses into overdrive. Her smell, the feel of her body against his, the taste of her kiss... They were all imprinted in his brain along with the memory of her blue eyes sparkling...

When she sighed again, his resistance cracked. Now that he'd found her, he wasn't letting go without a fight.

\* \* \* \*

Bliss flopped onto her back. She needed to wake up. Sleeping late wasn't her style, but then again, staying up past midnight wasn't one of her favorite things to do.

She opened her eyes. The room came into focus but wasn't familiar. Where was she? She drank in the details. Deep red walls and a black ceiling... Where could she have gone that had such dark colors?

An arm snaked around her waist, and she tensed. Bits and pieces of the night before rushed into her brain. Evan belonged to the arm around her. He belonged to the warm breath on her neck. What in the hell was she doing in bed with Evan Phillips?

Bliss eased the blankets up and peeked down at her body. Still fully clothed in the sleep shirt he'd given her. Odd. She glanced over at him. He wore a T-shirt and his sleep pants. He'd been a gentleman like he'd said? She wanted to believe her eyes, but she knew his track record.

She eased from beneath the covers and crept across the room. She needed air but didn't know the layout of the house enough to take a walk. Besides, what would his parents say when they saw her strolling through their home, if they were even there. She gazed out the window at the yard below. The chill of the morning nipped at her bare legs. She grabbed a spare blanket from the couch then plopped onto the window seat. Snow fluttered past the glass.

She mulled over the events of the last few weeks. Evan Phillips wasn't at all in her league. He belonged with pretty girls who had tons of confidence and perfect bodies. She didn't have a perfect body or lots of confidence. But she liked him. Every cell in her brain screamed to keep him at a distance, but something in her heart and gut said to see what would happen if she let him more fully into her life.

A thought niggled in her mind. He'd been the guy screwing her roommate while she'd slept above them on the top bunk. Good guys didn't do things like that. But he seemed as if he wanted redemption. Was he worth the second chance? He had been good to her. He'd helped her come out of her shell a bit and slept with her without expecting sex.

But was that out of desire or pity? Ben's rude remarks filled her head. He'd told her no guy in his right mind would be caught dead with her. Guys wanted women who put out and were willing to change.

She'd changed, but not because of Evan. She'd grown up. Would he treat her the same way? He kept saying he was a gentleman.

Trust him? Or keep looking?

She threaded her fingers into her hair. God, she was so confused.

"Do you always mutter to yourself when you gaze at the new-fallen snow on a crisp winter's morn?" Evan eased onto the cushion opposite her.

"Since when do you talk like you've stumbled out of a Lit book?" Bliss asked. In the morning light, she got a great view of Evan. His hair stuck out in odd directions, but the straight-out-of-bed look suited him. Magazines would pay top dollar for men who possessed half his charisma first thing in the morning. He embodied sex. Now she understood why he and Jessa were always screwing. Her nipples tightened, and her blood heated. She wanted to be the woman he didn't just sleep with, but the one he fucked.

"When I'm trying to impress a girl." He grinned. "You had me worried. I rolled over, expecting you to be there, and you weren't."

"I had to think." She wrapped the blanket tighter around her body to hide herself from him. "You said you'd be a good boy, but you were in bed with me." As much as she didn't want to fall under his spell, she couldn't deny the attraction.

"Did you mind?" He inched closer to her. "I didn't. It's cold up here. We shared body heat. Oh, and you're cute when you sleep. I couldn't resist."

"Evan." Her brain buzzed as she tried to keep up with everything he'd said. Cold, body heat…her being cute. "But you said…"

Why did he make her think of sex? She should be focused on the holiday, her studies or her living situation. Instead, she debated tossing the blanket aside and kissing him senseless.

"I'm a man of my word. I didn't try anything." His eyes glittered. Evan gathered her into his arms and tugged her onto his lap. "You were the one who snuggled into me. I'm not complaining. I slept better last night than I have in a long time. Guess I'm not made for sleeping on my own." He groaned. "This is a good fit."

"But you're made for sleeping with me? Or fitting together with me, as you say?"

"I am, and we are." He trailed his nose along her neck, drawing a moan from deep in her throat. "You make me want to be a good man, but for every pure thought, I've got a hundred ideas for how we can make each other very happy in a naughty way."

"Evan." She draped her arms around his neck. Might as well get comfortable. "Why are you doing this?"

"Doing what?" He fluttered kisses over her throat. "Kissing you? Holding you?"

"Teasing me." She pulled away from him enough to rest her forehead against his. "I'm serious. I'm not a trophy or a game to conquer."

"Good." He palmed her ass. "I'm trying to do this the right way by showing you I can change and that I'm attracted to you."

"You'll be the death of me." She closed her eyes and didn't get the chance to say more. Instead, he stole her breath with a deep kiss.

"Evan?"

Bliss froze. She'd heard his named called but didn't know the voice. She opened her eyes. "Your mom?"

"Uh-huh." Evan patted her butt. "Up. She'll come looking for me." He held her hand, keeping her close. "I don't care if she sees me with you. I've got nothing to be ashamed of and neither do you. But she's still my mom. Some things should be kept a secret." He turned his attention from Bliss. "I'm up here, Mom."

"When you're dressed, I've got a message from your coach. Breakfast is ready, too."

"You've got such a picture-perfect life." Bliss shrugged out of his grasp. "Are you sure there's room for me?"

"You're still doubting yourself." He nodded. "I don't know if my life is perfect, but it's getting better. Let's get dressed. I want you to meet my folks."

"Isn't that a little fast?" Then again, she was in their house. Bliss sighed. If she wanted to get out of the holiday funk, she needed to change her way of thinking. If he thought highly enough of her to bring her home and wanted her to meet his parents, then she'd welcome the opportunity.

"There's the smile I like." Evan kissed her again. "You're good for me, and I promise, you won't regret this."

"I'm sure I won't." She ducked into the bathroom and dressed in record time. The sweatshirt and jeans look wasn't her best, but she hadn't planned on actually spending the whole night with him. She emerged from the bathroom. "Evan?"

He stood with his back to her, talking on the phone. "I know, but I hadn't planned things that way."

She wrapped her arms around her body. Eavesdropping wasn't cool, but she wasn't sure where else to go. She crept up to him and tapped him on the shoulder. "Mom's in the kitchen. Go ahead down there. She won't bite." He turned back to the phone. "Yes, because pissing you off is my specialty. Christ. You think everything revolves around you. It doesn't."

Bliss left him alone with whoever he needed to argue with and went to the kitchen. She recognized Barbara in an instant. In person, Evan's mom looked even younger. "Hi. I'm

Bliss. Evan's on the phone. He said to come down here. Is that okay?"

Barbara smiled. "Okay? I told him to come along." She picked up a plate. "Sausage or bacon?"

"Bacon."

"I made scrambled eggs. They're Evan's favorite. Here." She handed Bliss the plate of food. "Gene will be in once he's done with the paper. He likes to read the whole thing cover to cover then eat." She sat at the bar with Bliss. "I hear you're an art major."

"Education. I want to teach elementary art." She stabbed a chunk of the eggs. "Thank you for breakfast. This smells so good."

"You've got a head on your shoulders. Good." Barbara sipped her coffee. "Evan's always been smart at school, but Gene wanted him to play ball. He's good at the sport, and I encouraged him to play, but I wanted him to have a career."

"Makes sense."

"What makes sense?" Evan's father strode into the room. "Oh, hello. Bliss?" His brows rose. "It's nice to meet you."

Now, she understood fully where Evan got his good looks. If that's how he'd look when got older, then sign her up. Save for a few small crinkles around his eyes and some silver hairs among the blond, he could pass for Evan's older brother.

"What time did you get in last night?" Gene sat on the other side of her. "Ev mentioned you'd come home with him."

"Around midnight." She toyed with the remaining eggs on her plate. Being stuck between Evan's parents seemed oddly weird and natural at the same time. Most of her wanted to get out of there with grace. The rest of her didn't mind the banter. At least, they wanted to talk to her. She could get used to having a family who cared. But which did she want? The family or the guy with the family? The memory of Evan holding her while she slept answered her question. Being accepted was nice, but she wanted him more, much more.

## *Chapter Seven*

Evan stomped into the room. "What a crock of shit." He slid the cordless phone across the counter. "I've got to go back to campus. It's a long story, but it has to do with the team. Bliss, want to ride along? I need to get a few things from the dorm, too."

He gritted his teeth. A million questions came to mind. How had Coach Murphy lost his paperwork? Sure, Evan didn't have to sort out the snafu just yet, but he hated to be late. Then there was the situation with Jessa. Pregnant? He knew better than to believe condoms worked every single time. The law of averages stated even the best protection wasn't foolproof and knowing Jessa… He'd been the fool.

She'd begged him to come back and insisted he needed to be there. She'd claimed he wouldn't regret meeting up with her. He pinched the bridge of his nose. Where in the hell did Jessa get the idea he was still interested? Sure, he'd step up if she was really pregnant, but if not, they weren't getting back together.

"I'm sorry. Bliss? It's up to you." His head ached. "You can stay here if you want."

"Sure. I'll come along. Thank you for breakfast. It was delicious." She slid off the barstool and hurried upstairs.

"What's wrong?" Gene filled a plate with eggs and sausage. "Trying to get rid of Bliss?"

"What? No." Evan plopped onto the stool Bliss had just vacated. "I made a bad decision, and it's coming back to haunt me. On top of that, my paperwork got screwed up. Knowing Coach, my stuff is on his desk and lost under one of his ten thousand play books."

"I see. I'll go check on Bliss. She might need some help." Barbara walked out of the room.

Evan waited for his mother to get out of earshot. Sometimes, a guy needed to talk to his Dad. "I'm so screwed."

"Jessa's pregnant?" Gene stirred his cup of coffee. "I told you about that crap, Ev."

"No—well, I don't think so. Jessa said she's late, but I'm not convinced. She's being clingy and not making any sense. This is way too calculated." His stomach churned. "I never should've dated her." He looked his father in the eye. "She said she'd come to the house on Christmas day if I didn't go back to the campus and sort this out. I don't want to ruin Christmas." Compound that with the crap from the team, and he wanted to scream. If he hadn't connected with Bliss, the whole semester would've been a disaster. Then again, once she found out about Jessa, she might kick his ass to the curb anyway.

"You've made the choice and have to deal with the consequences." Gene folded his hands on the counter. "I can't tell you what to do about Jessa. You knew her better than I did, but she's not my favorite person."

"I should've listened to you, Dad." He'd been bold enough to believe he knew everything. He'd been so immature and could lose Bliss.

"You've learned from your past, I assume, so go deal with the team issues and Jessa. Just make sure you're back before tomorrow. Bring Bliss, if she's still interested. I'm sure she'd like to spend Christmas with us. She seems sad. Don't make her even sadder."

Bliss. Damn it. She'd be even more upset when she found out he had to talk to Jessa. She'd kill him. He'd promised she could trust him. Now it would seem he'd been lying to her. He'd crush her, but if he left her at the house, she'd never forgive him.

Bliss came downstairs and crept into the kitchen. She clutched her coat and purse. "I'm ready. I could grab a couple extra outfits from Kade's." Her eyes widened. "He's my friend. He's gay. Not my boyfriend. I don't have a boyfriend. I mean. Evan and I didn't...we...uh... It's all platonic."

"It's fine, but I wouldn't say it's all platonic." Evan draped his arm around her shoulders. "Bliss is very important to me."

"You don't have to explain," Gene said. "I know Evan. He's a charmer." He waved. "Come back, Bliss. Barb makes one hell of a pumpkin pie. Don't goof off, Ev."

"I won't." Evan steered Bliss through the house to the back door. Once they were in the car, he sighed. He switched on the radio. Even if he'd have known what to say, he couldn't. The words had dried up, and his heart had lodged in his throat. He drove halfway to the campus before he finally spoke.

"Thanks for coming along." God, he sounded ridiculous, but he wasn't sure how to explain the situation. He didn't want to upset her. He liked Bliss and wanted to see her on a regular basis, not have her pissed before they even got started.

"Sure." She folded her hands on her lap. "What's the real story? Is there paperwork actually missing or is it something else?"

He snorted. She'd cut him to the quick. "How'd you guess?"

"I know you. You're a mess when it comes to Art History, but meticulous with baseball. You don't lose stuff, and you don't tolerate when the Coach screws up—even if it's paperwork that's probably misplaced." She stared at him. "Tell me the truth."

"Bliss." Even after a short period of time, she knew him. Why bother to hide from her? She'd stripped him barer than if they'd ripped off their clothes and fucked. Come to think of it, he wanted to have sex with her, too. He wanted to bare everything to her.

"It's bad, isn't it?" She folded her arms, bunching her breasts. "Fine. I left my stuff at your house. You can bring it back when you come to campus the next time. Just leave me at the student center."

"I never said I was leaving you there or anywhere else." He gripped the steering wheel. "That's the last thing I want to do. Why would you jump to that conclusion?"

"I'm jumping to that conclusion because I've got the world's worst guilt complex. If it's bad, it's got to be my fault." She glared at him, and the ice in her stare chilled him to the bone. "Instead of being the laughing stock, I'll bow out gracefully. Besides, who said it was up to you to decide my future? I'll be fine on campus or I'll find another friend to stay with, but I'll be on my own."

"Why would you do that? You have nothing to feel guilty for." He stopped at a traffic light and massaged his temples. As much as he wanted to get to the dorm and be done, he wanted to stop and reassure her. "I'm not leaving you alone on campus. There's no one here. No security and no staff. What if you have a problem? No one will help you." *Besides, my heart won't let me leave you there.* He continued forward when the light changed. "I refuse to leave you there."

"It's Jessa, isn't it? I can't compete with her," Bliss growled. "Look at her. She's perfect and beautiful. All she has to do is smile, and you boys all drop at her feet. I can't do that, even if I wanted to."

"There's no competition." *You've got her beat.* Evan wove onto the main street on campus to the dorm. "The situation with Jessa is complicated, but it shouldn't take long to sort out." He stopped in front of the dorm they shared. "Please. Just stay here."

"Jessa. Always Jessa." Bliss rolled her eyes. "The courtyard is behind the building. Going for a walk. Don't go looking for me."

"You know damn well I'll go looking for you. I'm not leaving you here alone." He knew she would be fine, but he refused to give up so easily. "Meet me back here in half an hour."

Bliss shrugged. She climbed out of the car then stormed around the building.

Evan groaned. He headed into the building, but the weight of the world pressed down on him. Once he talked to Jessa, he'd sort things out with Bliss and sign the paperwork for the upcoming season.

"Hey, Evan." Sherry, one of his former girlfriends, hurried across the foyer. "I didn't think you'd be here over break." She dragged him over to the mailboxes. "I heard you're on the market again, too. Think you've got time for an old flame?" She walked her fingers up his chest. "I've dreamed about another night with you."

"Actually, I'm not free." He clasped her hands. Time to play it cool so he could get away from her. "We had a good time, didn't we?"

"And we can again." She pressed his back into the mailboxes. "I want you."

"Sherry." He held onto her fists. "This isn't a good time." Why couldn't he say the words *I'm dating Bliss*?

"We can go behind the desk. I'm the only one back there for the next two hours. Plenty of time." She straddled his thigh and rubbed her groin on him. "Come on. Tell me you're free."

"He's free." Bliss stood beside them. "I knew it was too good to be true."

"What?" Sherry frowned. "What is she talking about?" She glared at Bliss. "You don't actually think he'll settle down enough to be good boyfriend material? I know him. He'll use you up then throw you away. He's a good time, not a forever man. Get the hint."

"Oh, I've got the hint. Goodbye, Evan." Bliss turned on her heel and strode away.

The moment she left him, his heart sank. Christ. What was he doing? Bliss meant the world to him, and he was wasting time arguing with one ex and about to placate another. He needed his head examined. "Look, Sherry, I don't do long commitments. I like being free, and I need to go."

"See, this is why I didn't want more than a hot time," Sherry said. "But you're going to go, huh? I don't think so. You just got here, and she dumped your ass. Let's go behind the desk so we can have fun."

"No." He eased out of her embrace. "I'm...I'm busy." Still not the words he wanted to say and hardly the truth.

She grabbed his arm, halting him. "Next thing you're going to say is you don't want to ruin the memories of what we shared by trying to do it again." She let go of him and rested her hands on her hips. "God. You're such a doofus."

"Me?" Evan groaned again. "I was about to say I'm seeing Bliss. Since she just left, I should be going, too. *Capisce?*"

"I understand, but I don't believe you. You're seeing her? She's awful," Sherry spat. "She's so plain. She's not even pretty. Why would you waste your time?"

"Not pretty? Who the hell are you to decide the standards of beauty? Your attitude destroys your looks." Evan shrugged away from Sherry. *She* was wasting his time. "She's the woman I need." He scanned the foyer, and the bit of the student common room that he could see. No Bliss. Fuck.

"You suck. You could've had me. Again. But you wanted the toad." Sherry flipped him off then slammed the door leading to the front desk.

Well, great. He hadn't wanted her, but also hadn't planned on ending things quite that way. Screw it. He needed to find Bliss.

Evan bounded up the stairs to the fourth floor. Unlike most days, the building was silent. His footsteps echoed off the walls. The place was almost creepy.

"Bliss?" Evan ran to her former room. "You in here?"

"Nope." Jessa stood in the doorway. She wore a thin T-shirt that showcased her lack of a bra underneath. Her nipples beaded. "I heard you talked to Sherry. She called me." She admired her manicure. "Come on. Bliss? Seriously? You can and have done so much better."

"Really?" Where did they all get off thinking they ran his life? "You wanted me here. I'm here."

"You were my best friend and I'm going through a traumatic time." Jessa slammed the door, closing him in the room. "Enough about the twit and Sherry. Let's talk about us."

"You said you were pregnant. How late are you?"

"Details, details." She pressed her body to his. "The real reason I wanted you here is because I know we're supposed to be together." She sighed and rubbed her crotch against his thigh. "The one time I told her to get a life and you walked out. What the hell is wrong with you? I know what you want. You need someone who can handle your lifestyle. That's me. Come back, and we'll forget the past."

"You're not late, are you?"

Jessa rolled her eyes. "You're supposed to be falling for me. Of course, I'm not late or pregnant. We couldn't have sex if I was."

She'd gotten on his nerves for the last time. "I came here for closure and the truth. You lied to me. You're the same snarky, mean girl I broke up with. I don't know what kind of lifestyle you think I have, but it doesn't include you or the money you think I'm going to make. Yes. We had crazy amounts of sex. We did, and it was passable. Now, it's over. You insulted my friend, acted like a shit and expected me to run to you when you cried pregnant. Well, this is it. I can't put up with your kind of…whatever this is. If you can't tell me the truth or think I'm crazy, then screw it. Forget me. Forget my number, my room, my face…all of it."

"You don't mean that." Jessa scowled. "You don't want us to be over." Her brows pinched together, and she pursed her lips. He'd once considered her beautiful. Now, he couldn't understand *what* he'd seen in her.

"God. I do. I never wanted to be with you long term. You cooked that all up in your head." He grasped the door handle. "I'm leaving with my dignity and my girlfriend. Don't get in my way."

He opened the door and stormed from the room. With each step away from Jessa, his dread melted away. He'd never considered himself spineless, but around her, he lost his gumption. No more.

Evan raced around the corner past the dorm room he shared with Rick. Just as he'd expected, Rick had left a note on the door.

*I'm out. Take care of Bliss or my bytes will byte your ass. She's a sweet girl and loyal. I'd date her if I wasn't with Kris. Later.*
*R*

Only Rick. Evan twisted the knob. Bliss said she'd gone for a walk. He couldn't expect for her to be waiting in his dorm room.

When he opened the door, his heart lodged in his throat again. *Please let her be there. Please.* Instead of finding Bliss, he found an empty room. His spirits drooped. She wasn't there. Damn it.

Evan gathered the clothes and the gear bag he'd forgotten. He'd be back in a little more than a week, but if he planned to go to the batting cages back home, he'd need his bats and helmet. A page of notes Bliss had written lay on his desk. He'd seen the notes a hundred times while studying, and he knew the words by heart. Something caught his attention. He grasped the paper and scanned the red lettering.

*You can do this. Focus and hit it out of the park just like in the baseball games you play. I believe in you.*

*Bliss*

Fuck. She'd... He hadn't even realized she'd written that.

Evan sagged onto the chair. His headache increased. Coming back hadn't been a bright idea. Yes, he'd retrieved his gear, but he'd lost the girl. The urge to punch something shot through his veins. Hitting anything wouldn't solve his problem. He needed to find his Bliss.

Evan chucked his gear and extra duffle bag into the hallway then locked the door to his dorm room. He picked up the bags and headed downstairs.

Where would she be? In the courtyard still? Maybe, but he'd been gone for half an hour. He ran through his options as he strode through the first-floor common area. The art building? Possibly. She'd had a painting class there last semester. Some of the students hung around and used the studio space. Kade's? Also possible. They were friends and she'd turn to him, no doubt. Could she get across campus that fast? He'd go to Kade's then make his way back to the art building. Either way, he had to find her.

# *Chapter Eight*

Evan bounded through the common area to the main desk, intending to go to the parking lot beyond it. He stopped short in the foyer. A lone figure sat on the one of the benches. Could it be her? Please, God, let her be there. He recognized the sweatshirt.

"Bliss." He whispered a prayer of thanks. "Honey, I'm so glad it's you."

She didn't turn around. He'd screwed up so much he didn't deserve any attention from her, but he still wanted Bliss.

"Bliss?" Evan bounded across the room and dropped his bags. He moved the hood from her head. "Thank God." He sat beside her and yanked her into his arms. "I thought I'd lost you."

"I'm not lost…just temporarily homeless." Her voice cracked. She wiped her face. "I wandered the courtyard, but it started to rain. I couldn't stand in the rain, so I came in here. Thought I'd ask about my room. Seems Jessa's got the dorm staff screwing me over, too. They said they lost my room transfer paperwork." She shuddered. Tears streamed down her face. "I never expected this to happen."

"What?" He gathered her on his lap. Having her back, even if she was pissed with him, felt so much better.

"I don't know where I stand with you. Part of me wants to smack you, and the rest…" She shook her head. "This isn't fair."

Evan smoothed his hand across her cheek to tip her gaze. The tears shimmering in her eyes brought out the blue even more. "I'm sorry."

"No." Bliss plopped her hand on his. She traced the lines of the veins in the back of his hand with her index finger. "You're the one I'm scared of. You've got a lot of play here."

"That's what's not fair?" He rested his head on her bicep. Her scent comforted him. "Talk to me."

"I like you, too. It's not fair. I want so bad not to be falling for you, but I can't help myself." A silent tear slipped down her cheek. "Awful, isn't it?"

"Not at all." They were on the same page. Thank you, God. He wanted to take her home and forget all about the campus, his exes and the rest of the world.

She stroked the hairs at the back of his neck. The move soothed him. "It sounds stupid if you think about it. I got here on a scholarship and don't have much. God. I'm so lame."

"You work hard for what you have. There's nothing wrong with that." He patted her hip. "Come on. We'll go to Kade's and get those clothes then we'll go back to the house. I'll settle the paperwork issue later."

Bliss stood. "Jessa told me why you came."

Evan didn't move. "I wasn't sure what to tell you."

"She said you wanted a second chance with her." She folded her arms. "Makes it hard to trust you when you can't be honest with me."

She was right, as usual. He'd once been told a liar can't make eye contact. He had nothing else to hide. Evan stared up into her eyes. "She called and said I needed to see her because she thought she might be pregnant. Call me stupid, but I fell for it. If I'd gotten her pregnant, I wanted to be sure. It doesn't seem like it, but I'm a man of my word. After I got off the phone with her, Coach called about the paperwork. He said it wasn't a big deal and I could sign the releases when I came back for conditioning. I lied and said that was the reason because I knew my folks would forbid me from leaving. I was scared to tell you because I like you. Not just flirting or because you're hot. I close my eyes, and I see you in my dreams. I can't wait until we spend time together. Even studying, which should be boring as hell, is fun because I'm with you."

She didn't say anything. The lack of communication knocked him off-kilter.

"I don't know what else to say to get you to understand. I'm baring my soul." Evan stood. "I don't have room in my heart for Jessa, but I do for you." Nothing else mattered. Not the holiday, the crap with Jessa or even baseball. For that moment, Bliss became his world.

"Evan." She rolled her eyes, but more tears fell. "What am I going to do?"

He caged her in his arms and petted her hair. "First, you're going to stop crying. She doesn't deserve your tears. Then you're going to cheer up. It's Christmas. We'll get your stuff from Kade's, if we can, so you'll have something to wear and then we'll go back to my folks' house. Tomorrow's Christmas Eve. You've got me until conditioning starts. When it does, come back here with me. We'll come up with something. Yeah?" One way or another, he'd convince her he wasn't a jerk and he was worthy of her love.

"Yeah." She gave him a half-smile. "Let's go back to your folks'. Kade's not here. He went home for Christmas."

"Are you willing to give me a chance—a second one? I like you, too."

"Here's to second chances." Bliss stood and wiped her face. "Let's have fun and make this Christmas one to remember."

His spirits and his heart leapt. He and Bliss were sure to fight again—everyone did—but they'd survived the first hurdle. When he looked into her eyes, he saw his future. Was that crazy? More than a little, but he liked what he saw.

Evan drove home as fast as possible but within the normal speed limits. He couldn't wait to get back to the house where the crap from school couldn't touch them. He held her hand, loving they way they fit together. He pulled into the driveway an hour later and stopped in front of the garage. The lights weren't on in the house. Had his parents gone away again? He climbed out of the car, rounded the hood then opened Bliss' door.

"Thanks." She blushed and yanked her coat tight around her body. "Time for another movie?"

"Something like that." Evan unlocked the door to the kitchen. Once she'd strolled into the house, he locked the door. "Mom? Dad?" He listened but got no answer. He peeked through the window into the garage. His father's BMW wasn't in the stall.

"Your mom left a note." Bliss handed him a piece of paper.

"Probably a party." He scanned the page. "Yep, they went to the Schwitzer's. Down the street. I grew up with their daughter, Dirinda. Nice people." He sighed. "I'm glad. I didn't want to face them right now." He turned his attention to Bliss. He wanted to repair the damage between them, first.

"Now what?" She shrugged out of her coat and clutched the garment in her arms. "Do you want to go to the party?"

"Nope." Evan locked the door. He took off his coat and place both his and hers on the hooks by the door. "I want to get some food, watch some television and hang out. We'll have a Christmas Eve party tomorrow. Come on." He switched on the oven. "Let's see what's on the cable channels." He steered Bliss toward the living room and flipped the switch to turn on the lights.

"Wow." Bliss stopped short. "I didn't realize there were so many Christmas lights in here. It's like a magazine."

"Mom loves Christmas." Evan wrapped his arms around her. He'd seen the lights so many times, but never really noticed the marvel of the glittering colors. Looking at the room through Bliss' eyes changed his perceptions. "If it's red or green, she'll put it up."

"It's romantic," she whispered.

"It is." He kissed her neck. "Very." God, he wanted to be naked with Bliss, right under the Christmas lights.

"Evan." She sagged in his embrace and rubbed her ass against his groin. "I'm supposed to be mad at you."

"You're supposed to be leery of me." He nipped her neck again, this time right below her ear. "Hating my guts."

"You're horrible for me." Bliss grasped his hands but didn't push him away. "I shouldn't be here."

"Nope, but you are." He turned her around in his arms. Her eyes widened, and a thin ring of blue shone around the black. Deep red stained her cheeks, and she'd parted her lips. Evan slid one hand under the back of her shirt. "I want to make you feel good. Want you to care for me the way I do for you."

"Evan." She closed her eyes. "We can't. Not here."

He'd said he'd be a gentleman. He wouldn't push her. "I want to make love to you under the Christmas lights."

Bliss froze. She clutched his hands. "I've never—Evan."

She was a virgin. He remembered her telling him that bit of information. His hands shook and tingles shot all around his body. He wanted to be the one to make love to her first.

He needed that connection with her. "Do you trust me?"

Bliss opened her eyes. A tiny voice in her mind screamed not to trust him. Good God, he was lousy for her. He'd screwed her roommate, but he'd been so sweet since. Was the change an act? The same dick-headed guy who'd spent so much time in her dorm room wasn't the same one who worked like hell to memorize Baroque paintings and offered to bring her home for the holidays. He could be doing so many nice things to get into her pants, but she doubted that. Down in the pit of her stomach, she trusted him. Probably not smart, but she wanted to try everything—with him.

"I do trust you," she murmured. "Take me upstairs."

Evan nodded. He strode past her into the kitchen then after a moment he returned.

"What...?"

"I turned off the oven. No point in making food just yet." Evan offered his hand. "Come with me?"

Bliss tossed aside her fears and followed him to the second floor. Her heart beat wildly, and her skin prickled. If someone had asked her at the beginning of the school year if she thought she'd have a boyfriend or lose her virginity over the course of the year, she wouldn't have said no.

He tugged her to the bed and collapsed with her on top of him. Evan wrapped his arms around her again. He kissed her, nipping her bottom lip. He swallowed her moans and sucked on her tongue.

Every bit of her heated straight through. Getting naked with him scared her, but she wouldn't let her doubts control her. No more looking back. She sat up on his lap and grasped the hem of her sweatshirt. She yanked it over her head. Her T-shirt clung to her body.

Evan stroked her sides and belly. He drew circles on her ribs with his thumbs. "So beautiful."

"I haven't taken my shirt off." She held her breath and hiked the thin cotton over her head. Her ponytail flopped onto her shoulders. The chill in the air curled around her. She shivered.

Evan sat up, with her still on his lap, and slid one hand into her hair. He tilted her head and kissed her. When he took control, her entire being vibrated. She balled her hands on his shoulders.

"Touch me, babe." Evan kissed along her jaw to her ear then bit her earlobe. "Talk to me. Tell me I'm making you happy."

"You are," she whispered.

He hummed and dragged his nose down her cheek. "I want to please you." He popped the clasp on her bra, loosening the lingerie.

Instead of yanking the garment off her chest, he kept the bit of lace pinned between them.

If she didn't relax...

Bliss blew out a long breath. She didn't want to miss a moment. She unclasped her hands and threaded her fingers into his hair. She rested her forehead against his.

"Like this?" Evan rocked her on his lap. The bulge in his jeans rubbed on her pussy, despite the layers of denim between their bodies.

"Yeah." Bliss wiggled, allowing the bra to fall away from her chest. She stared into his eyes. "Evan."

"Beautiful." Evan licked a path of fire from her chin, down her throat to her collarbone. "Love." He palmed one of her breasts and held her tight to his hips. "Damn."

She'd reduced him to one word sentences. Nice. She leaned back in his embrace enough for him to see her breasts. "Touch me."

"I am." He smiled. "I'm going slow." Evan cupped her boob in his hand and sucked on her nipple.

The new sensation excited her. She'd always know her breasts were sensitive, and his caresses with his tongue pleased her.

"Evan," she moaned. "Wow." She tugged on his hair. "More."

He swirled his tongue around her areola then scraped his teeth across her nipple. She pulled harder on his hair then forced herself to let go. The more excited she got, the harder she yanked. Not to the point of actually hurting him.

He switched to her other breast. More nipping, licking and sucking. Her brain swam. She'd masturbated, but touching herself hardly compared to what he did.

Evan patted her hip. "Stand up."

"I don't know if I can." She wobbled to her feet. "I'm weak in the knees."

"I'll hold you." He kept one arm around her and buried his face in her chest. At the same time, he popped the button on her jeans.

Bliss gasped for breath. This was really happening. Despite being half nude, her skin sizzled. She should've been chilly. She hooked her fingers into the waistband of her underwear. With Evan's help, she shucked both her jeans and panties.

"Are you wet for me?" Evan dragged his tongue around her bellybutton. "Bet you're so wet."

Her panties stuck, and when she tried to step out of the damp garments, she tumbled forward. "Sorry."

"Are you falling for me?" He chuckled then placed her on the bed. "God, you're so…"

"I'm what?" She grasped the sheets, ready to cover her nudity. A pang of embarrassment hit her hard.

"Sexy." Evan knelt at the side of the bed. He parted her thighs. "Smell so good." He parted her pussy lips. "You're drenched for me." He slid his fingers up and down her slit.

Bliss tensed. She'd used her vibrator to get off plenty of times, but nothing compared to the predatory look in Evan's eyes or the heat of his breath on her pussy.

"I've dreamed about you." He opened her to his gaze. "Wanted to taste you for so long." He dragged his tongue along her pussy lips.

The feather-light touches teased her. She shivered. From deep in her cunt to her nipples, she felt his caress. Holy shit. She tensed her hands. Did she want to cover up? No. She wanted to expose everything to him.

Evan slipped one finger into her cunt. "Wow. You're so tight."

Her skin prickled again, and perspiration popped out on her chest.

"Feels good?" Evan nipped the inside of her thigh. "Talk to me. I like to know if I'm pleasing you."

"I…more." The rest of the words escaped her. Her legs trembled, and she shifted her hips. She couldn't breathe.

"Touch me. Pull my hair," Evan said between licks. "Come apart for me."

She grabbed one of his hands and placed his palm on her breast. Evan pinched her nipple. He rolled the tight bundle of nerves between his fingers, matching the rhythm of his licks with the pressure on her breast.

"Evan," she cried out. She squeezed her legs together. Everything trembled. The heat in her belly exploded and spiraled through her veins. "Oh my God."

"That's so fucking sexy." Evan removed his finger and lapped at her juices. "Come for me, babe. Yes."

She shuddered. No matter how hard she tried, she couldn't catch her breath. The room spun. She sagged on the bed. Her arms and legs refused to cooperate. She closed her eyes.

Evan eased her legs closed. He crawled onto the bed beside her and tucked her to his chest. He kissed her temple. "Merry Christmas, babe."

Merry Christmas, indeed.

# Chapter Nine

Evan nuzzled her neck. Seeing her come apart turned him on. She responded to him so well. Each murmur and whimper spurred him to want to be a better man for her. He'd fallen for her much earlier, but being with her made him understand how much he truly cared. She flowed through his soul.

"Evan?"

"Right here." He kissed her again. "Like that?"

"I felt like I was flying." She rolled onto her side, facing him. "I'm tingly."

"Being with the right person will do that." He wasn't sure if he was talking to her or himself. He'd convinced himself he didn't deserve Bliss, but he was wrong. She'd brought him out of his funk, and even when she annoyed him, he couldn't turn away. He craved her. Crazy, since they hadn't even fucked yet.

"Make love to me." Bliss crawled on top of him. Her hair slipped over her shoulders.

"Slow down." Evan rolled her underneath him. He'd make love to her, yes, but first, he wanted to move at a more leisurely pace. He stood and removed his shirt. Her eyes gleamed, and she tugged the blankets over her body.

"Cold?" he asked. Evan shoved his jeans and boxers to the floor. When he stepped out of the wadded up fabric, he tripped and fell forward. He managed to catch himself before he landed on her.

"Cold and excited." She grinned. "Looks like you're falling for me, too."

"I am." He kicked out of the cumbersome fabric then stood tall. His cock bobbed and pre-cum glistened on the tip. He'd thought he'd been in love — whatever love was — a couple times, but no one had swept him off his feet like Bliss. He stroked himself twice then reached into his nightstand for a condom.

"You're prepared, too." She smiled then took the foil packet from his hands. "Let me." Although she struggled with the packet, she finally opened the rubber and sheathed him.

Having her hands on his body was like heaven. He groaned and rocked into her curled fingers.

"Antsy?" she asked. Her sweet smile melted him even more.

"For you? I am." Evan crawled on top of her. He clasped her hand, linking their fingers. "There's no way I can make this not hurt. Focus on me." He reached between their bodies and lined up his cock up with her pussy lips. Her cream would help lube the way, but he'd still have to stretch her.

"Arms around me." Evan kissed her. He could lose himself in her kiss and happily not surface for a while. She relaxed beneath him. "Good girl," he murmured and locked his gaze on hers. He eased his dick into her body, centimeters at a time.

Bliss kept her gaze on him, but her brow furrowed. Her lips twisted in a frown, but she didn't cry out.

"I know, babe. I know." He kissed the corner of her mouth. "Relax and focus on me." He pushed into her more. Her lips parted, and she whimpered as he pushed past the resistance of her hymen. His heart ached as she squeezed his fingers. "The pain won't last long," he said. Evan braced himself on his forearm and buried himself balls deep in her pussy. Instead of moving and thrusting right away, he lingered to allow her time to adjust to him.

"Evan," she managed. She closed her eyes and dug her heels into his lower back.

"You're doing great." He sounded like a ridiculous coach, but whatever. She *was* doing great. "You grip me so tight. I want to stay inside you forever."

Bliss opened her eyes. "Make love to me."

"I am." Evan feasted on her mouth, loving her sweetness. "Put your arms around me." When she did, he rocked his hips. He moved in and out of her until only the tip of his cock remained inside. She dug her fingernails into his shoulders and gritted her teeth. Fuck. He'd wanted to make their first time memorable, but not because he'd hurt her.

He increased his speed. Damn. The heat flowing through his veins, and the building orgasm weren't to be denied. He nipped at her throat. "Still with me, Bliss?"

"Yeah." She gripped him tighter. "Keep going."

"It will get better." He bumped noses with her. "Promise."

"I believe you."

The sincerity in her voice and her trust buoyed him. He picked up even more speed, thrusting into her. The synapses in his brain misfired, and his entire body sizzled. She made his heart beat and permeated his thoughts.

"Bliss," he bit out. "Jesus." The rest of whatever he wanted to say faded, and rational thought left his brain. He moved on sheer instinct and adrenaline. His thrusts turned feral. "Mine," he whispered. "All mine."

Evan slammed into her pussy and groaned. He deposited seed deep in the condom. Holy fuck. At least, the rubber was there as a barrier. He sagged in her arms and panted. She hadn't come this time, but he'd gotten the hurting over with. He'd work on getting her to come next time. Climaxes weren't fun when they were solo.

After a few moments, he pulled out and rolled onto his back.

"I'm not a virgin," she whispered. A tear slipped down her cheek.

"Nope." Evan wobbled to a seated position and removed the used condom. He chucked the rubber into his waste bin then stretched out beside her again. "I don't want to sound like a dick, but stand up." When she did, he draped a blanket around her shoulders. "I need to clean this up."

He removed the soiled comforter from the bed and retrieved another comforter from the closet. "It's not sexy to have to make you get up, but it's better than the alternative." He turned back the sheets and comforter. "Let me get you a washcloth."

"I can do it." Bliss darted past him and disappeared into the bathroom.

He glanced down at his belly and groin. She'd bled, but not as bad as he'd expected. He debated running the soiled bedding down to the laundry, but didn't. He'd worry about the wash in the morning. Right now, he wanted to focus on her and making sure she was comfortable.

Bliss crept back into the bedroom. "Ten minutes ago, I was on fire. Now, I'm freezing."

Evan patted the mattress. "Jump in. I'm good at heating things back up." He palmed her ass as she passed him again. Once she'd climbed under the covers, he settled beside her. He rested his arm on her belly. "Now's the best part—holding each other afterward."

"I like this part." Bliss snuggled in his embrace. "You weren't kidding. You're good at warming me up."

If she wiggled too much more, she'd have him rock hard again. He dragged a long breath into his lungs then exhaled and kissed her shoulder. "You were wonderful."

"I was?" The sparkle returned to her eyes. "It did hurt. I knew there would be blood, but I didn't think it would be that much."

"I'm sorry. It gets better with practice, and yeah, I want to keep practicing with you. After a few times, it won't hurt. Promise." He tangled his legs with hers. "Did you like it—besides the whole pain and intensity?"

"Sex?" She smoothed her hand over his cheek. "I don't feel any different—other than being sore. But I liked it." She dragged the pad of her thumb across his bottom lip. "I expect you to keep practicing with me."

"Absolutely." He brushed the tear from her cheek. She'd been a trooper. He didn't know how much the first time hurt, but he'd been told it was massive. She'd shown her discomfort but wasn't running off screaming into the night or swearing she'd never fuck him again.

"When was your first time?" She drew circles on his cheek with the tip of her index finger. "And something random. Do you have to be clean shaven for the baseball team?"

Talk about two totally different topics... "We have to be presentable for baseball. I shave, but I assume you like the whiskers?"

"I do," she said in a low voice. "But you're handsome either way."

"Thank you." Evan sighed. From his head to his toes, relaxation claimed him—or was it her claiming him? Maybe both. He spread his hand out on her hip. "You asked about my first time. I was eighteen. I'd been dating Chrissy for almost four months. At the time, I wasn't planning on having sex. We'd gone to prom and were leaving when she said she wanted to take a detour. Me, being naïve and not the sex-starved jock everyone thought I was, went along with her suggestion. Her parents owned property around the outskirts of town. All farmland, since her dad was a farmer. Anyway, we parked at the end of the gravel lane separating four great big corn fields. She told me she loved me and gave me a blowjob." He chuckled. "I came too fast, and she laughed at me. When I was ready to go again, she fucked me on the driver's seat of Dad's Beemer. Thank God, he traded the car."

He'd blocked out most of his first time. Chrissy had been a nice girl, but nothing more than a high-school crush. She hadn't wanted forever with him any more than he'd wanted to stick around town for the rest of his life.

"Anyway, that was almost four years ago. I'm glad I went through the experience." Although, he wished he could've waited for Bliss. "This sounds mean, but I haven't thought about Chrissy in a long time."

Bliss cuddled tighter to him. "You said you were going to be a gentleman with me. You also said you wouldn't push. Kinda looks like you made your way around the bases and stole home plate."

"Is the umpire calling me out?"

She shook her head. "Totally safe."

Evan laughed until his chest hurt. He loved the way she could make silly baseball puns and didn't take herself seriously. "Will you come to my games?"

"Watch you whack a ball around a field and stand in the outfield to scratch? Or are you the player that has to tap everything and scratch before he hits the ball?"

"I have to adjust my uniform, but I'm not a human rain delay." Although, he'd been known to run through a battery of superstitious actions before he stepped into the batter's box. He curled his fingers under her chin. "Why? Does that make a difference?"

"Not really." She grinned. "I'd go to the games pretty much no matter what you did. Support for the home team is always welcome, but if you think I'll be there so you can show off, you're wrong. I won't be supporting the jock. I'll be supporting you."

"This is why you're good for me." He held her close. Money, potential fame and the material crap didn't rock her world. She liked him for the real man inside. He closed his eyes and saw a flash of his future—him and Bliss standing on the front porch of a brick house. In his vision, he wore a badge with a school emblem on it. Which school, he wasn't sure. She propped a baby on her hip and waved. Yeah, he wanted to marry her one day. Was he putting the cart before the horse? Maybe, but he'd been accused of being a romantic before. Why not accept the truth?

"Why'd you wait so long to lose your virginity?" Evan opened his eyes. "Did you have some kind of vision that I'd be the right guy?"

"Not a chance." She giggled. "When you first walked into the room with Jessa, I wanted to throw something at you. I hated your guts."

Just as she'd built him up, now, she managed to tear him down a little. "My ego needed deflating. Thanks."

"I don't think you actually saw the inside of the dorm room. You only saw Jessa and the bed." Bliss shrugged. "But when I got to know you, I realized you're still a horny toad, but you're a good man who acts like a horny toad sometimes."

"Guilty as charged." He sighed. All the energy drained out of him. "For you, I'll work to be that better man."

"I know you will." She draped her arm across his chest. "You asked about my virginity. I didn't wait because I somehow saw you in my dreams or anything like that." She shrugged. "When you're the weird girl at school, guys don't look at you. I wasn't even cool enough to be that girl who was one of the guys. I didn't exist."

He wanted to say something, but wasn't sure what to add to the conversation. Apologizing seemed like pandering, and empathizing was ridiculous. He hadn't been at her school, but he'd been one of the guys who never really noticed the world around him. He saw only the pretty girls.

"I had crushes on two guys—Eric and Ryan. Neither of them was interested. Ryan was all tangled up with Crystal. Eric dated a girl named Mandy. When they wanted someone to talk to or to discuss problems in their respective relationships, I was good enough. For anything else? Not a chance. I went to my junior prom alone and only ended up going to senior prom with Ben because I thought he was my boyfriend."

"You thought he was? Did he lie?" He couldn't imagine a guy would lead a girl on like that, but then he'd met some real jerks.

"I was told one story and the rest of the world knew another. The rest of the school was in on the joke. Kinda like Carrie, but without the blood. He said he liked me, took me out and showed me off at prom, but all the while, everyone was laughing. It turned out he wanted to screw me because he had a list and boxes to check off. I didn't matter to him."

"What an ass." Evan stroked her arm. Now, her reactions made sense. How she'd managed to put up with him and Jessa, why she'd accepted the screaming and her ability to see the change in him. "You've got a good heart, babe. I'm glad you're letting me in."

"I wasn't kidding when I said don't hurt me," she whispered.

"I'll do my best never to hurt you again." He meant every word. He tucked his free arm behind his head. He respected her so much. Even if it took the rest of his life, he'd be the man she needed.

"Night, Evan."

"Goodnight, babe. You've given me the most precious gift tonight." He closed his eyes and drifted to sleep with thoughts of making love to Bliss filling his mind. She'd been everything he wanted and more. The gold bracelet he'd purchased hardly made up for her gift to him, but he didn't mind. He'd had the best Christmas ever, and the holiday wasn't even over with. Down to his soul, he belonged to Bliss.

# *Chapter Ten*

Bliss stared at herself in the mirror in Evan's mother's bedroom. She didn't look any different, but she felt like a new woman. She still ached from sex the night before. Every time she moved, she thought about laying with Evan. The blossoming relationship with him could be dangerous. He kept saying the right things and acting so sweet, but part of her still didn't trust him. She smoothed the wrinkles in her dress. How could she trust him enough to have sex with him, but not enough to offer up her heart?

"You look wonderful." Evan's mom stood behind Bliss. "He said you cleaned up nicely, but he was wrong. You're a stunner." Barbara fluffed Bliss's hair. "Smile. It's Christmas Eve."

"I'm happy."

"Truly?" Barbara hugged her. "I've see the way Evan looks at you. He might not know it yet, but he's in love."

"I don't know. I'm not sure he knows what he wants." The glitter on her cheeks caught the light. Part of her wanted to change back into her comfy sweatshirt and jeans. The rest of her wanted to knock Evan off his feet.

"Men never know what they want. That's why we have to work so hard." Barbara handed Bliss a gold necklace. "You need one more touch to make the outfit complete. There." She draped the chain around Bliss' throat. "I see why he likes you. You see through his bullshit."

Her eyes widened. She hadn't expected his mother to swear.

"It's true. He likes to act like a tough guy. I understand why his father wanted him to play ball, but I also see how it turned him into a jock. You keep him level." Barbara nodded. "Having that D in art history brought him back to earth. I shouldn't be, but I'm glad."

"The information was there, but he needed help getting it all straight."

"He's saving you, too. Getting you out and about, making you smile. Don't let that light within you go back out. Let him in." She squeezed Bliss' shoulders. "He's waiting downstairs for you."

Bliss swallowed her shock. She hadn't expected his mother to accept her quite so easily.

Weren't mothers supposed to suspect the girl their son brought home? Maybe, she'd hit the jackpot and found a great guy with an equally great family.

She brushed her hair off her forehead and started toward the stairs. Her heart thrummed against her ribs. Evan had seen her in the cocktail dress, but anxiety still filled her mind.

She descended the stairs. People she didn't know milled through the house. Knots of partygoers stood together, conversing. No one seemed to notice her. She wandered into the kitchen, not sure where to find Evan. Being around so many people she didn't know wasn't awful, but it also wasn't her idea of fun.

"Hello." A guy she'd never seen before stood next to her at the counter. "You must be one of Evan's cousins."

"No."

"Huh." The man frowned. He didn't appear much older than her. The green flecks in his eyes sparkled, and his red hair glinted in the light. "Have I talked to you before?"

"I don't think so." Her skin prickled, but not like with Evan.

"Wait. You're Ev's girlfriend, aren't you?" He narrowed his eyes. "You don't look like the girl he described. She was taller and skinnier."

Her cheeks heated. "That's Jessa."

"Right." His eyes widened, and he nodded. "Now, I recognize you. You're that girl from the party on campus. You're Jessa's crazy ex-roommate. Did you honestly watch them have sex? Was she hot?"

Her stomach soured. How could one person be so vile? She'd only been at the Christmas party for a few minutes and already wanted to hide upstairs.

"Did you?" He stepped in her way. "It's always the fat chicks."

"I'm not fat," she snapped. "Move." She shoved him out of the way then realized getting physical wasn't exactly ladylike.

"Bliss?" Evan appeared beside the red-headed guy. "What's going on here? Lucas, what did you say?"

Shit. The tips of her ears burned. He'd seen her get upset. She wanted to disappear.

"Nothing." Lucas shrugged. "We were talking baseball."

"What?" She pressed her lips together. She wasn't going to give Lucas any more rope. No way. Maybe if she kept quiet, they'd forget she was there.

Evan narrowed his eyes and tipped his head to the side. "Gonna go with that? Or think of something more intelligent?" He stood between Bliss and Lucas. "You stuck your foot in your mouth, didn't you?"

She figured Evan would stand up for her, but still, hearing him actually say the words floored her. Her love for him swelled a bit more.

"Well, she's not hot like Jessa. God. You can do better." Lucas curled his lips in a sneer. "And to have her come to your parents' party? Dude, we have friends here."

Her pride deflated. Lucas was right. She wasn't a beautiful girl like Jessa. Her skin prickled, and she scanned the room for an exit. She needed to get out of the stuffy place.

"Some more than others." Evan stuffed his hands into his pockets. "Okay, here's how this is going to go. You're going to apologize—"

Apologize? She forgot about her need to leave and stared at Evan.

"Right. Tell me you're sorry and leaving," Lucas interjected. He turned his attention to Bliss. "Like right now, right?"

"No," Evan growled. He stepped between Bliss and Lucas again. "You, Lucas, are going to apologize to my girlfriend, Bliss. Then you're going to leave her alone."

Shock shot through her. He'd stood up for her…again.

"Now wait a minute. We've been best friends since second grade. You're going to take her side over mine?" Lucas snorted. "She's so not your type."

"Maybe, I had to find my type to know what I wanted." Evan blocked not only Bliss' escape but also Lucas' access to her. "Apologize. You're lucky I haven't told you to leave."

"The guys from the team are here." Lucas grabbed Evan's arm and yanked him out of Bliss' earshot.

She couldn't make out what they said over the noise of the party. Just as well. She didn't really want to hear anything else Lucas had to say.

"There's our left fielder." Another guy joined Evan and Lucas. Then two more gathered around the three.

"That's my cue," Bliss muttered. She turned on her heel and walked out of the kitchen. She could stand up for herself all day long, but why bother when she was outnumbered? She maneuvered through the house to the den where one of the five Christmas trees had been set up.

White lights twinkled on the painted white branches. Ornaments featuring baseball players, baseballs and other paraphernalia concerning baseball decorated the faux-fir tree. A beaded wreath ornament caught her attention. In the middle of the wreath was a photo of Evan. She guessed he had to be about ten or eleven. His blond hair flopped over his forehead despite the hat he wore, and one of his front teeth was missing. She smiled. Even at a young age, he was handsome. She reached out to trail her fingers over the beads.

The floor creaked. Bliss stopped short of touching the ornament and froze. The person behind her shut the door and clicked the lock. The scent of woodsy cologne curled around her, and she didn't have to look to see who'd joined her. Evan.

"You didn't have to leave." He eased up beside her. "Lucas is a dick. He's always been a dick."

"Did you ever think he might be right? About you and I not being suited for each other?" She shrugged, trying to act nonchalant. "In a way, he's on the right track. I feel so out of place here. I'm scared to touch most everything for fear I'll break it. This is the only nice dress I have, and I don't even own a necklace to go with it. This one's your mom's."

"So?" Evan leaned on the arm of the leather sofa. "Lucas was wrong."

"Are you sure?"

"Completely." He patted his thigh. "Come here."

Bliss hesitated but eventually closed the gap between them.

Evan yanked her between his legs but allowed her to stand. "Just because you have stuff, doesn't make you a better person. Look at all the crap Jessa has stowed in your old dorm room. She's got the room overflowing, but her attitude is shit. Yes, she's pretty. I won't lie—she is, but her beauty is cancelled out by that temper of hers."

"Thanks for the pep talk." Bliss tried to wiggle away from him, but he held her tight.

"Lucas is a lot like Jessa. Yeah, we've been good friends for a long time, but it's because of the team. If I hadn't played baseball, I doubt I'd have hung out with him. He's a douche. You thought I went through women like toilet paper? He's worse." He placed his finger over her lips. "Before you give me another snappy comeback, give me a chance. He never, ever should've talked to you like that. Whether you've got a dollar or a million dollars, he's not the judge. He's also got a big mouth. Just because you think I'm handsome, doesn't mean everyone does."

"You're joking, right?" She sighed. Her damn low self-esteem wouldn't go away. "I know how the girls on campus look at you. I heard them whisper when you and Jessa walked past. They all want you. It's kind of lewd the way they talk about offering themselves up just for a chance to be with you. But they aren't with you; I am. I know I'm not going to win any beauty pageants. It's a matter of time before you come to your senses and realize you can and should be doing so much better." She'd said more than she wanted to, but at least, she'd spoken the truth.

"Babe." He cuddled her to his chest and stared up into her eyes. "I didn't realize how much work I have to do."

His words stung. She tried to keep her hurt at bay, but the anger, frustration and tears welled to the surface. God. Why did she have to crumble now? Because she felt like a project. He'd do something nice, build her up and then dumped her like everyone else. Her mother, her father, Ben... Maybe, she was the reason they'd all left.

"What are you thinking?" Evan cradled her jaw in both hands. "I can't read you."

"Nothing." She blinked back the tears, swearing they weren't going to fall.

"Bullshit." Evan tipped her gaze, forcing her to look into his eyes. His brows knotted and a pair of creases formed between his eyes. His jaw muscle twitched. "You're hurting. Talk to me, and don't you dare tell me it's nothing."

"I've never been enough. Not for my parents, not for my one shot at a boyfriend, not for actual friends or even a bat-shit crazy roommate. I try to be myself, and I'm too weird or ugly." The words poured out of her. "I just want to be enough. Not almost, not sort of, but enough." Her voice cracked. She closed her eyes to keep from completely falling apart.

"I misspoke." Evan rested his forehead against hers and cradled her skull in his hands. "When I said I had a lot of work to do, it wasn't— I wasn't trying to insult you. I meant that building you up so you can see yourself the way I do is going to be a challenge, but it's worth the challenge. Ryan, Eric and Ben were nuts to pass you up, but I'm glad they did. You're everything I could ever want. You're smart, beautiful—despite my jackass former friend's assumption—and the sweetest woman I've ever known. I keep hoping you don't realize I'm the one who doesn't deserve you."

She wanted to snap at him, but didn't. As much as she didn't want to believe him and wanted to wallow in her self-pity, she trusted him. God, she was screwed up.

"One of these days, you'll believe me. Soon, I hope." Evan smiled. "I really like you and want to keep you in my life." He pressed his lips to hers. "Besides, it's Christmas Eve. No one should have to cry on Christmas Eve."

The tears fell. She'd tried to keep them at bay and failed. She'd spent many a Christmas upset and hurting, but usually, no one paid her any mind. Evan cared. Even if she couldn't wrap her mind around how he cared, he did.

He kissed her again then brushed his nose against hers. "My friends are turds. Don't let them bother you." He arranged her legs so she straddled his thigh. "They wish they were me and had you on their side."

"You're making that up, but I appreciate it." She draped her arms around his neck. "Thanks, Evan."

"No need to thank me yet. I haven't given you your present." He patted her ass. "And I promise it's not just sex. In my coat pocket. Grab the box."

Bliss did as he asked. She pulled a long, slender box from inside his coat. "What's this?"

"Open it."

When she cracked the lid, her breath lodged in her throat. A gold chain lay atop the dark-green velvet. In the middle of the chain, a heart charm dangled. Letters had been engraved on the shiny charm.

"MVP?" she asked. "Trying to say you're the best baseball player, and I need to know it?" She managed a smile.

"I'm not the MVP. You are. Most valuable person, player, partner…you name it, but that's how I see you." Evan plucked the chain from the velvet. "Here." He affixed the bracelet around her wrist. "Merry Christmas, babe."

"Thank you." She admired the jewelry. "This is more than I could've asked for."

"Then I picked out the right present."

"Evan… I didn't get you anything this cool. I emailed Rick about helping me cobble something together for your computer."

"More memory?" Evan asked. When she nodded, his eyes lit up. "Between the play books and the papers I have to write for class, I'm running out of memory. It's perfect. Thank you." He kissed her wrist then rubbed the charm with his thumb. "Santa brought me what I wanted — you and don't you dare say I got the raw end of the deal. I'm the king of the world because I've got you in my arms and extra memory for the computer." His eyes sparkled, and his voice dropped to a husky growl. "Kinda makes me want to ditch the party and take you upstairs to show you how much I appreciate my gift."

"Horny toad."

"You know it, and you're the reason. You make me want you all the time." He swatted her butt. "You're my girl."

She grasped his shoulders. For the first time since they'd gotten together, she didn't see him as just another guy or the dream man she happened to be friends with, but as hers. They were a pair. She'd let go of the past concerning her issues with her parents. It was time to let go of the past with guys, too. Evan wasn't Ryan or Eric and certainly not Ben. No more mistrusting him.

"What do you say? We make our excuses to my folks and blow this popsicle stand?" Evan hiked up her skirt. "God, I want you."

Bliss nodded. "I want you, too."

He'd locked the door, but the chance someone might come looking for them spurred her on. She dropped to her knees between his legs. She'd only ever given a hand job once — which had turned out disastrously — but she'd seen porn and know what to do in order to give a blowjob. He'd given her pleasure beyond anything she'd ever imagined.

Time to do the same for him.

# *Chapter Eleven*

Evan slid his fingers into her hair. Holy God, she was going to blow him. "Wait." He shook his head. "Not here. Let me sit." He scooted over to the couch and sprawled out. "I'll fall off the arm of the chair otherwise."

"Oh." Innocence shown in her eyes. "Sorry." She tucked her hair behind her ears then licked her lips.

"You wouldn't know." Evan stifled a groan. "Not a problem."

Bliss slid her palms along his inner thighs, sending shivers through his body. She massaged his cock through the fabric of his trousers and boxer shorts. He balled his fists. He needed to let her control what happened, not push her too fast. He wanted her to enjoy the moment.

She stared up at him. "I'm nervous."

"You're doing fine." He held out his hand then clasped her fingers. He eased down in his seat. "I like it."

She kept her gaze on him but moved from his thighs to the bulge growing behind his zipper. Each touch and caress both pleased and tensed him. Even though he'd locked the door, someone could knock on it at any moment.

Bliss tugged down the zipper on his pants then popped the button. The release of pressure helped improve his situation, but not much. She licked her lips again then eased his cock through the gap in his boxer shorts. Her eyes widened.

She'd seen him naked, but he understood. Looking at something from afar wasn't always as impressive as right in your face. "Take your time," he murmured. "We've got all night."

Bliss wrapped her free hand around his shaft and stroked. A low growl started in his throat. He tipped back his head but continued watching her. Oh damn. Heat started low in his belly and radiated down his limbs. His cock twitched.

Although her eyes were still wide, she smiled. She leaned forward. While stroking him, she flicked her tongue along the blunt head of his erection.

"Babe." He gritted his teeth to keep from shouting. Everything she did felt good. "Take me in."

Bliss opened her mouth. She bobbed her head, taking more of him between her lips each time until she'd engulfed him completely. She glanced up at him and nodded.

"You're...wow." Evan shivered. He fought the urge to take over. He slid his fingers into her hair. "A little faster, babe."

Bliss grasped his knees and rocked back and forth. She sucked him deep into her mouth then let go. Her teeth raked over his shaft.

"Not so much teeth." He guided her, fucking her mouth at the same time. When she swallowed against the head of his cock, he groaned. "Damn, that's good."

His brain buzzed, and his legs trembled. He needed more. Evan tipped his head to the side and cradled her head in his hands. He bucked his hips. She'd done a wonderful job, but she had him so close. He bit back a moan and panted. Fuck.

Bliss reached between his legs and stuck her fingers beneath the bunched fabric of his pants and boxers. She caressed his balls.

"Fuck." His restraint broke. He surged forward then withdrew and let go of her head. "I'm coming."

Bliss crawled closer to him and sucked him back into her mouth.

"Babe." Too late. No matter how hard he tried, he couldn't hold back the orgasm. Evan shuddered and emptied his seed into her mouth.

He gasped for breath and sagged against the couch.

"Was that good?" Bliss eased up between his thighs and tucked his cock back behind his pants. She didn't zip him, but rather smoothed her hands along his abs. "That's the first blowjob I've ever given."

"I'm happy." Evan adjusted his rumpled boxers and pants then zipped. He fought to catch his breath and reached for her. "Come here."

She climbed onto his lap and rested her head on his shoulder. "It tasted strange. Not bad, but strange."

Evan laughed. He'd never thought about what cum tasted like. He cradled her in his arms. He wanted to stay right there in that moment with her forever.

"Think anyone noticed we're gone?" Bliss asked.

"Nah. Mom asked me to make a token appearance. I did." He stroked her bare arm. The bracelet caught the light and sparkled. He touched the charm. "I was planning on heading out tomorrow night. I want to lift and practice at the school. Will that work for you?"

"Yeah, but that's a pretty quick change of subject." She clasped his hand. "I don't mind. I wanted to run to the bookstore downtown, so I'll have something to do."

"Want to watch me in the cages? I can teach you to play." He turned enough to look into her eyes and bobbed his eyebrows. "Learning to bat properly can be pretty sexy. Me right behind you with my arms around you."

"Holding that hard wood in my hands?" she asked and gave him a sideways glance. She grinned. "I'm sure that's very hot."

"Smart ass." He cupped her jaw and kissed her. "This is why we're together. You get me."

"I've got you, all right." She giggled. "But I understand."

"Ev?" His father knocked on the door. "You in there?"

"Yeah, Dad." He smothered a laugh behind his hand. "Need me?"

"Is Bliss in there with you?"

"Yeah." He dropped his voice to a whisper. "Sorry. I never expected him to come looking for me." He wiped his hand across his mouth and swallowed back another chuckle. "Did you need me?"

"Your Aunt Beth is here and wants to see you. Your mother wants her to meet Bliss." He knocked again. "Think you can tear yourselves away from each other long enough to say hi?"

"We can." Embarrassment washed over him. He should've known someone would want him around. "Give me a few."

"Don't goof off."

Evan patted Bliss' hip. "We've been found out." When she scurried off his lap, he stood. "Good thing Dad's got a mirror in here." He backed away from the glass and checked his look in the reflection. He adjusted his trousers and fixed the tuck in his shirt. "Come here." Evan swiped his thumb across her bottom lip. "I'm a mess, and you're still beautiful."

"I didn't do that much." She finger-combed her hair from her face. "At least, I wasn't wearing lipstick."

Evan kissed the side of her head. "You'd be beautiful no matter what. Merry Christmas, babe."

She slid her hand into his then kissed him back. "Merry Christmas to you, too. Let's go meet the family."

* * * *

The next night, Evan climbed into the car and sat beside Bliss. Together, they'd suffered through the numerous introductions and conversations with friends and family. He'd kept Bliss at his side. He'd rubbed her back and kissed her. Each time she'd tensed, he'd whispered in her ear. Well after midnight on Christmas Eve, they'd finally crashed. He'd wanted to make love to her that night, but didn't. They had the rest of the semester together.

"Ready to head back to the pressure cooker?" he asked and grasped her hand. He kissed her knuckles. "I'll see what the schedule is, but I may not be able to get into the rec center until tomorrow."

"No problem." She smiled. He liked that he'd gotten her to do that more often—smile and relax. "Think we've got time to go to the bookstore? I'd rather ride than walk, and the busses aren't rolling for another week."

"Sure." Evan drove to the campus, but instead of going straight to the dorm, he zipped down the main street to the shops downtown. The trip from his hometown of Oleana to Kenton took two hours, but he barely noticed the time. Bliss grabbed too much of his attention. He parked in front of the store and switched off the engine.

"I don't know about you, but I love the smell of old books." Bliss clapped her hands. "Books for me are like baseball for you."

"Hours of entertainment that some people equate to watching paint dry?" Evan asked. "Nah, I get it. I don't like to sit still that long, but I understand."

Bliss left the car and practically bounded into the store. Evan hung back a few paces and watched her. She moved with enthusiasm. He followed her to the art section then to the romance novels. She trailed her fingers over the spines of the books until she found whatever she'd come looking for.

He'd never pictured himself standing in the bookstore, perfectly content to be waiting on anyone, but when he was with Bliss, he felt complete.

"I've got what I wanted." She grinned. "Three trashy paperbacks and the Greek art book for my portfolio review." She paid for the books then returned to the car with him. "You're supposed to do your writing course this semester, right? If you need research help, I know the library like the back of my hand."

"Cool and yes. I will need help." He draped his arm around her shoulders. "Reading the books will no doubt put me to sleep."

"Some of that stuff can be boring." She shrugged away from him when he opened the car door.

Evan rounded the hood and plopped beside her on the seat. He liked that they had easy conversation. The sex was off the charts, yes, but they worked well in the real world, too.

"I'm scared to death to do my portfolio review. Since I'm lower in seniority in the class, I'll probably have to go early in the semester." She clutched the bag. "Gets it over with faster, though."

"True." He sped back to the campus and parked in the lot by the dorm. A few other cars were already there. He didn't see Jessa's red coupe. Hopefully, she wasn't back yet.

"You don't have to do a review per se, but don't you have to demonstrate you can do the sports you want the kids to play?" Bliss asked. She fell into step beside him and helped haul the bags into the dorm. "They can't play dodge ball all the time."

"No, they can't. If the physical education teacher knows his or her stuff, he or she is skilled in most sports. Doesn't mean I have to be great at all of them, but you're right. I need to know the fundamentals. I've taken classes for the major sports—football, baseball, soccer, volleyball, basketball and billiards. Okay, billiards isn't considered a major sport, but it was a fun class. You play pool for pretty much the entire class session."

"The most exciting class I took outside of my Art Ed classes was the Lit class based on the Vietnam war." Bliss ducked under his arm as he held open the door to the fourth floor.

He chuckled. He'd ascended the stairs without realizing what he'd done and without breaking conversation. Nice. He stepped back a pace and watched her ass wiggle as she walked. His mouth watered. Damn, she had a nice ass. Just enough to grab during sex and the right amount of jiggle to entice him.

Bliss stopped in front of Evan's door. "Looks like Rick *is* gone."

"You doubted me?" Evan shoved his key into the lock and opened the door. "You're the one who had him fix my computer."

"I did, but he never mentioned future plans. He was too busy telling me about gigabytes and asking if Kris really liked him. I've only known her for a year. I have no idea if she was that in to him or if she was just being nice."

Evan plunked his bags on the floor. "Well, my room is your room until you're sick of me." Hopefully, that wouldn't be for a long time. "I have some noodles and rice, if you're hungry."

"I'm okay for now." Bliss placed her bag next to his then stepped up to the window. She sighed. "The campus is so pretty, all white with snow and no footprints. It's almost dreamlike."

"I guess it is." He'd seen the campus plenty of times, but never thought about it as pretty or dreamy. It was a collection of buildings and roads. Seeing the place through her eyes changed his outlook. "For the next few days, it's pretty much all ours, too."

"I know." She leaned back in his arms and rested her head on his shoulder.

"I've got time to practice in the cages without some of my team members hogging the space. You've got time to read, and we've got New Year's Eve to experiment." He squeezed her. "See how many sexual positions we can try before the ball drops."

She laughed and snuggled in his arms. "You're a horny devil, but I must be, too, because that sounds like fun. You do have enough rubbers, though, right?"

"You doubt me?"

"Nope, but if I can't give you hell, who can?"

"Spoken like we've been together forever." He breathed in the scent of her hair. She intoxicated him. "Since I mentioned sex, I'm dying to be inside you." He turned her around in his embrace and feasted on her mouth. Bliss opened to him right away. She sucked on his tongue and slid her hands beneath his coat. The garment eased down his shoulders and arms then plopped onto the floor.

Evan made quick work of divesting her of her coat then collapsed on the bed with her beneath him. He palmed her breast through the fabric of her sweater and situated his knee between her thighs. When she moaned, he swallowed the sound. They didn't have to be quiet, but he also didn't want to share the experience with anyone but her.

He rolled onto his back, pulling her onto his chest. Without breaking the kiss, he grabbed the hem of her sweater and her undershirt. He'd waited long enough to be with her again. He needed his woman.

"Evan." Bliss sat up and yanked the sweater and shirt up over her head. The move left her in just her bra from the waist up. She placed her hands together on his chest, which bunched her breasts and made the straps of the bra slide down her shoulders.

"Now that is fucking sexy." Evan reached around her and opened the clasp. The lingerie puddled around her wrists. "Better than in my dreams," he said. He sat up and caressed her back. Bliss closed her eyes. A lazy smile curled on her lips, and her nipples beaded.

Evan held her closer and sucked on her breast. He drew circles around her areola.

"Oh, wow." She toyed with the hairs at the back of his neck. Each light tug sent shivers down his spine.

He groaned. Foreplay would have to wait until later. Evan popped the button on her jeans then tugged both the denim and her underwear down around her ankles. He placed her on the bed. Bliss fixed her gaze on him as she untied her shoes, then kicked out of the footwear and wadded up fabric.

"There is something so sexy about a woman in nothing but a pair of socks." He ripped his shirt up over his head. "I'm hooked."

"You're silly." She propped herself up on her elbows. Her pussy lips glistened with cream. Ready for him?

Evan's cock jabbed against the zipper of his jeans. He shoved the fabric down his legs. The denim plus his boxer shorts gathered at his ankles. Instead of stepping out of the clothing, he grabbed a condom from the nightstand and sheathed himself. The time for getting properly naked would have to wait until later.

"Evan!" Bliss giggled as he tackled her on the bed. "You'll rip something."

"I don't care." He lined up his dick with her pussy then tweaked her clit once he sank into her. When she yelped, he clamped his mouth down on hers.

Bliss gasped and dug her fingernails into his shoulders. She turned her head to breathe, allowing him to nip at her throat. She brought out the wild in him. The soft touches and sweet lovemaking would have to wait. He needed her now.

Evan pumped his hips, sinking deep into her then retreating. She clamped down around him, adding to his pleasure. The springs squeaked with each thrust.

"Feels so good," she panted. "You're going to kill me. I'm dying in your arms."

"You like it." He buried his face against her neck. He wasn't sure how she could be so eloquent. His brain had turned to mush the moment he'd filled her. Perspiration prickled on his back. His body heated, and every nerve ending sizzled. He couldn't think and just moved on instinct. Nothing mattered but her.

"Evan." She met him thrust for thrust. "Oh my God."

He shuddered. The orgasm rolled around in his belly. Until she cried out, he'd thought he could keep the climax at bay. Not any longer. He shoved himself deep into her and grunted. He poured his seed into the condom. Holy shit.

"Come for me," he bit out. "Come apart."

She said something he couldn't understand then shivered beneath him. She tightened, holding him inside her. Her breath feathered over his cheeks as she relaxed. A chuckle vibrated from her throat, and she gazed up at him from under heavy-lidded eyes.

"I'm floating," she murmured.

"A good orgasm will do that."

"Uh-huh." She kept her arms and legs around him. She didn't say anything else for the longest time. Instead, she held him. When she did finally speak, she sighed. "I get it."

"What?" He braced himself on his forearms and rested his forehead against hers. "What do you get?"

"Why you did all that shouting. I tried to keep quiet, but I lost all control." She petted the hairs on the back of his head. "Even without the bracelet or the trip to your folks' house, this has been the best vacation of my life."

"Yeah?" He kissed her. "Mine, too." Evan pulled out of her and ditched both the condom and his wrinkled clothes. He kicked his shoes out of the way then settled in bed with her. Bliss curled against his side and placed her hand over his heart.

Within moments, her breathing evened out. She tangled her legs with his.

Evan grinned and closed his eyes. Words he'd never thought he'd say teetered on the tip of his tongue. He kissed the top of her head. Why not admit the truth? Maybe, she'd even hear him. He wasn't ashamed of his feelings. Hell, he wanted to shout from the rooftops that he'd found the woman who made his heart beat.

Just before he drifted to sleep, he murmured his exact thoughts. "I love you, Bliss."

## *Chapter Twelve*

Evan toweled off his forehead. In the two months since Christmas, he and Bliss had been almost inseparable. When he wasn't in class or conditioning for the baseball season, he made time for her. Call him crazy, but he preferred her company to that of his teammates or most of his other friends. Rick came by the dorm room from time to time, mostly to experiment on the computer and to talk about his own girlfriend, Kris.

Evan tossed the towel onto the bench of the weight machine then rested his elbows on his knees. He couldn't wait to get back into the batting cage. He'd figured out if he changed his stance just a little and leaned into the pitches a bit more, his batting averages improved.

He also couldn't wait to get back to Bliss. Their date nights were probably considered boring by the standards of his friends on the team. She brought food back from the cafeteria, they watched movies and made love. Her sex drive matched his.

When they weren't screwing like rabbits, as she'd put it, they worked on their respective studies. He'd watched her complete the oil crayon drawings for her portfolio and even posed for a couple of the works. She helped him with the papers he'd written, by proofreading and checking them. Together, he and Bliss were a great match.

He scrubbed both hands over his face. He needed to get his head back into baseball. The games weren't far off, and he had to be ready to play.

"There he is." Lucas wove around the weight machine and folded his arms. He stood in front of Evan. "You're our new clean-up hitter."

"So I've been told." Evan rolled his shoulders then stood. "It's a good fit." Although he had been surprised to see his position elevated in the hitting order.

"Good?" Lucas snorted. He shook his head. "Should be me."

"I've got to go to the batting cages." Evan brushed past Lucas. He'd had enough of his teammate's complaining. Every day, Lucas bitched about the lineup. For God's sake, the hitting order could and would change, depending on who had a hot streak going and which pitcher they were against.

He strode into the locker room and grabbed his gear bag from his locker.

The trip across the building to the batting cages didn't take long. Evan embraced the silence along his walk. He knew just how competitive the team could be. Most of the guys were being scouted by the professional teams. Because he had no intention of going pro, he didn't have the same pressures. His thoughts turned to the outline for his first paper for his history and philosophy class. He needed to head back to the library later that day to get better info on the history of baseball and how the sport had been integrated into school physical education curriculums.

He donned his batting helmet then picked up his favorite bat. Evan waved to the student assistant running the automated pitching machine. He ran through his battery of stretches then stepped into the batter's box. Of the thirty-six pitches, he connected with twenty-eight. Five ended up being foul balls, but most were easy line drives and lobs.

"Your hitting has improved." Xavier, another teammate, grabbed the chain link wall of the cage. "Want to let me in on the secret? My averages suck right now." Of the guys on the team, Evan liked talking to Xavier most. He didn't pull punches and played fair.

"I'm happy. That's the whole deal."

Xavier curled his fingers in the links. "Happy? Are you referring to the reason Lucas is having a fit?"

"My position in the batting order isn't the reason." Evan strode out of the cage and leaned his bat against the back wall of the prep area. He removed his batting gloves and helmet. "I'm on the team. That's an accomplishment."

"Not for you. Dude, you're one of our best hitters without your secret to success. I still don't get why you're not letting the scouts know you're interested in going pro."

"I'm not." Evan tucked the gloves and bat into his gear bag. "No desire to go into the majors."

"Really?" Xavier snorted. "I thought you did."

Lucas strolled into the prep area. "Thought he did what?"

Evan rolled his eyes. "Xavier, if you want to lob baseballs, I need the fielding practice. Are you game?"

"Sure." Xavier grabbed his gear bag. "Lucas? You in?"

"Can't wait." Lucas kept up with Evan and Xavier. "Did Evan tell you who he's dating?"

"Who is it this month?" Xavier asked.

"It's not who. It's what." Lucas chuckled. "Ev, I swear, you could've picked a better looking chick. One who's way sexier than the one you've got."

"What's wrong with her?" Evan asked. He opened the door to the indoor football field. The space allowed for longer throws, and balls could be hit the approximate distance of the baseball field. "She's sweet."

"She's ugly," Lucas spat.

"Who?" Xavier stuffed his hand into his glove. "I'll catch first. I need the practice."

"Bliss. She's... I like who I'm becoming because of her." Evan grinned. "She's good for me. Keeps me balanced."

"Translation: she's a dog and boring as hell." Lucas gripped the baseball. "She doesn't stand out in a crowd, and she won't help your image."

"Go fuck yourself," Evan snarled. He didn't give a rat's ass about his image. That had been his problem. Until a very short time ago, he cared too much about what other people thought. Once he'd let go of that hang-up, he liked himself better. Besides, he refused to allow Lucas to verbally abuse Bliss, even if she couldn't hear him.

"I bet she's a virgin, too." Lucas laughed. "God, she's lame."

Evan gripped the baseball bat. If he wasn't careful, he'd do something he'd regret that would also get him tossed off the team.

"Is she?" Lucas asked. He narrowed his eyes. "Bet she's never even seen a dick."

He was lowering himself to Lucas' level, but fuck it. "No and no." He turned away from Lucas. "Xavier, go long. I need to work off some frustration."

"You got it." Xavier hustled away from Evan to the far end of the field. Only Lucas remained close.

"Then she was a pity fuck. Whoever did her — and I'm including you — didn't do it because they wanted to." Lucas whipped the baseball bat through the air, taking a swing at an invisible ball. "Was it a pity fuck?"

"You're a dick, Lucas. A fucking huge dick. Leave Bliss alone, okay? She's my girlfriend, and she makes me happy. If you don't like it, find Jessa and date her or whatever it is you want to do." Evan heaved the baseball into the air then swung. The crack as the bat connected with the ball, echoed in the room. The white ball sailed toward Xavier.

"Nice hit," Xavier called. "Again?"

Evan tossed another ball into the air. Once again, he connected and sent the ball arcing toward where Xavier stood.

"I think I *will* date Jessa. She's way hotter than Bliss, and I hear she's not seeing anyone."

Lucas shrugged. "I've always wanted a trophy girlfriend."

"Have at it." *And good luck.* Evan lobbed another ball in Xavier's general direction. *What a prick.* Although he didn't want to think about Lucas, the nasty words stuck in his head. He didn't care if Lucas disliked Bliss, but was this ribbing a means to mess with his game? Lucas said he wanted to be the clean-up hitter. Would he stoop to teasing in order to get his way? Probably.

Evan hit ten more balls to Xavier. His back ached from swinging the bat and reaching for the ball. "Ready to switch?"

"Don't know if I can hit them all that far out," Xavier said as he hustled up to Evan. "You're on fire."

"I'm mad."

"About Lucas? He's an airhead." Xavier dropped his glove onto the turf by his bag. "Don't let him get to you. He's always had a thing for Jessa and has wanted to be you since we started college. He's a good player, but he doesn't have the spark you do." He shrugged. "He worries more about getting into the majors than he does about having his degree when he's done with college. You know what Coach says."

"If you don't have a degree to fall back on, you'd better hope you're headed for the Hall of Fame because you won't have shit if your ball career stalls." Evan chuckled. "He's right."

Xavier paused next to Evan. "Let me ask you this. Bliss makes you feel like the world's best ballplayer, doesn't she? Like as long as you've got her on your side, you're golden?"

"Pretty much."

"Then screw Lucas and his ridiculous jealousy. You've got a good thing going." Xavier slung the bat over his shoulder. "Ready to work off that anger by catching a few line drives?"

"Sounds like a plan." Evan hustled out to the middle of the field. Xavier was right. Lucas didn't deserve his anger or the time of day. He dragged a long breath into his lungs and let it out slowly. *Eyes on the ball. Eyes on the prize.*

By the time he finished fielding the balls hit in his direction, Evan's body ached. He'd pushed himself harder than he'd planned to but was glad for the effort. His thoughts turned to his paper. When he had to talk about the fundamentals of the sport, he could with gusto because he'd immersed himself in the game.

Evan rolled his shoulders again. "Thanks for the workout."

Xavier nodded. "Any time. Plan on tagging me the next time we've got to double up. I'm tired of working out with Jonesy. He's a nice guy, but man does he swear a lot."

"Sounds like a plan." Evan strode into the locker room. He hurried through a shower then dried off and changed clothes. He checked the watch he'd tucked into the front pocket of his gear bag. Nearly five. Damn. He'd told Bliss he'd be back to the dorm at five so they could go to the library together. He zipped the bag then shoved his arms into his coat. If he cut across the commons by the student center, he'd shave a few minutes off the walk.

He stuffed his hands into his coat pockets then left the rec center. The chilly air stung his cheeks and the tip of his nose. He could've driven, but then he'd have lost his parking spot by the dorm. Not a horrible trade-off, but why waste the gas when he needed the exercise? Fat snowflakes fell around him. At least, the ground wasn't covered.

Ten minutes later, he stomped through the front door of the dorm. He shook his head, sending snow all over the floor.

"Hey." Jessa bounded up to him. "Guess what." She clasped her hands together. "You're going to love this."

"I doubt it. Look, I don't have time for guessing games. I've got to get upstairs to change." He sidestepped around her and unlocked the door to the stairwell.

"Evan. I'm with the baseball team." Jessa kept in time beside him. "I'm the scorekeeper."

"You? You hate math." He continued up the stairs. "I thought Hayley was doing it."

"She decided to quit college. Something about getting pregnant. Anyway, the job is mine. I get to travel with the team and attend the major practices. Aren't you excited?" Jessa squealed. "I'm thrilled. I can't wait."

"I can." He brushed past her and headed down the men's hallway on the fourth floor.

"No goodbye?" Jessa called.

"Nope." Evan slid his key into the lock then turned the knob. "Honey, I'm home." When he glanced down the hall, he noticed Jessa's confused stare. *Good. Let her be confused.* He closed the door. "Bliss?"

"Right here." Bliss stretched out across the bed. Instead of being covered up in her standard sweatshirt or the blanket, she'd covered her body in his baseball jersey. She'd only tucked her feet under the covers. Her bare legs shimmered in the harsh dorm room light. She propped herself up on her elbow. Her hair spilled over her shoulders in fat curls.

"Wow." Evan dropped his gear bag with a thud. "This is so much better than coming home to Rick."

"Is it?" She sat up then braced herself on her knees. The shift in position revealed her lack of undergarments. She'd left the jersey unbuttoned to her navel. Only a pair of pink panties were visible under the jersey. "I wanted to surprise you when you got home from practice."

"I'm definitely surprised — in a great way." He shucked his coat and kicked out of his running shoes. "Hot damn." He flicked the knob on the door, engaging the lock.

"You look tense." She toyed with the remaining buttons. "Need some help relaxing?"

"I've got just what I need." Evan scooped her into his arms then turned around and sat on the bed. He positioned her legs in order for her to straddle his lap. The jersey bunched and slid off her shoulder, revealing her bare breast. "How did you know I'd want to make love when I got back?" He pressed his face to her chest and breathed in the sweet scent of her perfume. He kissed her boobs then focused on her nipples.

Bliss draped her arms around his neck. "I wanted to make you happy."

"You are," he said against her breast. He eased the jersey the rest of the way open and moved the garment off her shoulders. "This is the best. You bare and all mine."

"I am all yours," she said, her voice low. She cupped her boobs, giving him better access. "I like when you nip them."

He sucked her nipple into his mouth then eased one hand into the elastic of her thin panties. She'd gotten more brazen and trusted him. He didn't want to let her down. With each touch, he fell harder for her. His desire grew.

"Evan, faster." She stilled his hands. "Make love to me."

"We'll never have slow, sweet sex." He held her in his arms. "But I can't get enough of you."

"Me, neither."

Evan stood with her in his arms and placed her on the bed. He let go of her long enough to remove his shirt and to shove his pants and boxers to his ankles. The garments waded up around his feet, but he managed to free himself. He grabbed a condom from the box beside the bed. No need to put them away. Hell, they made love so much he hadn't bothered to conceal the box. He tore the packet, unrolled the rubber then sheathed himself. No matter how fast he moved, he couldn't get to her quickly enough.

Bliss opened her legs and reached for him.

He loved this woman—more than he could possibly understand, but he loved her. Evan stroked himself then entered her. The moment he filled her to the hilt, he paused. Her eyes glittered, and pink infused her cheeks. He'd never seen anyone so beautiful.

"You're staring at me." She clutched his shoulders. "Evan?"

"Admiring you." He planted his knees and arranged her legs on his thighs. Although he started off slow, his thrusts increased. He pumped into her, loving the way she gripped him. Her lips parted, and she smiled.

One day, he's slow down enough for them to both savor the moment. Not today. He nipped the corner of her mouth. With all his soul, he belonged to her.

Evan rolled his hips, filling her then pulling most of the way out. When he was with her, he was home. No stealing, no hoping. He knew.

Bliss shivered beneath him. "Evan." She dug her fingernails into his upper arms. "More."

Evan picked up the pace. Sweat prickled down his spine, and his thoughts fuzzed. The rest of the world, his troubles, his triumphs…everything faded away. He embraced the heat spiraling through his veins and gave in to the orgasm.

"Holy shit," he said through clenched teeth.

Bliss tensed and squeezed her eyes shut. A tiny whimper escaped her lips. She drew her knees together then relaxed. She gasped for breath. "Now, I get it."

Evan braced himself as best he could to keep from crushing her but didn't pull out. "What do you get?" Besides his love and devotion.

"Why people want to have sex so much." She opened her eyes. "If you're with the right person, it's explosive."

"I found the right person." Evan cradled her beneath his body. She understood what he wanted to do with his life and supported him. She'd become everything he needed and more than he could ever desire. Forget the crap from the team. Soon, he'd be done with his time at Kenton, but he'd never be done with Bliss.

## *Chapter Thirteen*

Bliss shivered on the bleachers. The calendar read April, but she swore the temperature gauge had the wrong information. Who played ball in forty-degree weather? She wrapped the blanket tighter around her body. Her cheeks hurt from the stinging cold air. Thankfully, she and Evan had plans later that would make up for freezing her ass off.

Once the game concluded, she and Evan were going to meet his parents for supper. Evan wanted to celebrate her passing her portfolio review. She smiled to herself. She'd never expected to be so happy. If she didn't know better, she'd have said she was in love.

Was love possible? Especially at a young age? She'd barely experienced life. How could she know if she'd found the person she wanted to spend the rest of her life with? She smoothed her hands across her belly. Down in her gut, she knew. She'd fallen in love with Evan Phillips.

She turned her attention back to the game. Earlier in the inning, Evan's sacrifice fly out to left field got a runner home and allowed the Eagles to pull ahead. Xavier stepped up to the plate. Of Evan's teammates, she liked Xavier the best. He treated her with dignity. Some of the players saw her as an interloper. Not Xavier. She encouraged him to keep following his dream to the major leagues. According to Evan, scouts for some of the teams were in attendance and looking at Xavier. Unfortunately for Xavier, his pop fly landed directly in the glove of the right fielder and ended the inning.

On the plus side, the game was over, the Eagles triumphant. She sighed and gathered up her seat cushion, the blanket and her purse. Bliss headed to Evan's car first and unloaded her things.

She grabbed his bottle of cologne. Evan had called the room before she'd left for the game and asked if she'd bring the items he'd forgotten. She stuffed the bottle into her purse and made her way back to the clubhouse.

Five years before, the team had won a grant to improve the facilities. To make the grounds more fan-friendly, they'd had a fan zone built. She wasn't permitted into the players area so she waited in front of the trophy case.

Some of the players filtered out of the locker room. Xavier waved and wandered away with his girlfriend, Tricia. Bliss waved back. If Xavier was changed, Evan shouldn't be far off.

She heard voices. Jessa strolled into the fan zone, but she wasn't alone. She yanked on Evan's arm.

"Come on. You need to come to the party." Jessa stopped Evan. She pressed her body to his. "It's a victory party. You're the hero."

"I hit a sac fly. It's not that great." He nudged her away. "I've got plans."

"No, you don't. I talked to Lucas. You're going to dinner. Big deal. Take me with you then come to the party." Jessa grabbed the front of Evan's coat. "What? Are you going to hang out with Bliss? You've moved on from her."

Evan's jaw muscle twitched, and he glared at Jessa. Bliss hung back. He had to deal with Jessa on his own. If she stepped in, she'd emasculate him. Plus, he was in a public place. If any of them caused a scene, everyone in the fan zone would know.

Jessa glanced over in Bliss' general direction. She must've seen Bliss because her eyes narrowed. Jessa yanked Evan close again. She smashed her mouth over his. He didn't push her away, but he also didn't seem to enjoy the kiss.

Bliss strolled up to them and plunked the bottle of cologne in Evan's coat pocket. She didn't say a word before she walked away. She straightened her shoulders and left the building.

The bus heading back to campus waited in front of the fan zone. Bliss stepped onto the vehicle. She wasn't mad at him. Wasn't hurt by Jessa's actions. Honestly, she understood. Crazy, but she did. Jessa wanted what she'd lost and thought this was the only way to get him back. Bliss also realized how easily temptation could sway Evan's judgment. What if she hadn't been there? She trusted him, but any man could fall off the beaten path.

She grasped her purse as the bus rolled toward campus. A million thoughts swirled in her brain. In the last few months, she'd grown up. She wasn't the shy girl who allowed people to walk all over her. She'd learned about sex and love. She'd even passed the two major tests to get her teaching license. She wasn't in a good place with her family, but she knew who she was and what she wanted out of life.

When the bus stopped at the dorm, she nodded and exited the vehicle.

"There you are." Evan bounded up to her. "I could've gotten a ticket racing up here. Why did you leave?"

"Jessa." She should've been upset, but wasn't.

"You're not still worried about her? God. She pushed herself onto me." Evan thrust his hands into his hair. "She's a pain in my ass."

"I know, and I'm not worried." Bliss kept her voice even.

"I don't—" Evan paused. The venom left his voice. "Wait. You're not? Then why did you leave?"

"Part of the deal is that I'm worried about you. A tiger can't change his stripes. You and Jessa were together a short time, but you burned pretty bright. It's normal for her to want you back and for you to maybe wonder what could be if you tried things again. I trust you, but I'm also not dumb." Being honest freed her. She'd held too much in for far too long.

"I'm not interested in her." Evan folded his arms. "Irritated but not interested."

"I believe you." She'd always sort of known he wouldn't run off with Jessa. Still, her doubts about herself lingered.

"Then? There's got to be more to this than just your worry," Evan growled.

"Maybe, we need a break to know what we're missing." She stood firm. She loved him but wasn't sure if he loved her in return. Everything had happened so fast. Could the feelings they shared be that strong and last?

"Bliss." His shoulders slumped, and the frustration left his voice. "What are you saying?"

"I need some time to think. I know your folks are here and we're supposed to celebrate, but maybe, we've moved at light speed. We've been attached at the hip." She gripped her purse strap. "I need to be sure this is what I want."

Evan unfolded his arms and stuffed his hands into his jacket pockets. He stared at her and furrowed his brows. "I've got an away game tomorrow. We'll be gone until Sunday afternoon. Will that be enough time or do you need more?"

"It'll be a good break." At least, she hoped it would be.

"You're breaking my heart." Evan plunked the keys to the dorm in her hands. "I've got to go." He paused. "Bliss, I've been in your shoes. I've had my share of relationships where the girl walked. She broke my heart and the bitterness made me not want to have another girlfriend. That's why I just dated. Then I met you." He touched her cheek. "Jessa has never been the one I wanted."

"No? You screwed her enough." She'd been meaner than she'd planned. Damn it.

"I made a mistake," he said softly. "I learned. You made me slow down and see what was great about being a couple."

"Evan." Her heart splintered. He knew how to say the right things and act so sweet.

"Please. Don't shut me out. I love you, Bliss. More than I thought I could. Please believe me." He bowed his head. "I'll give you the space you need, but don't take forever."

"I do believe you. That's why I'm scared. My heart knows who it wants, but in my head, I'm not so sure." Her eyes burned with unshed tears. She trembled. He'd said he loved her, and she believed him, but taking that last leap seemed almost impossible. Something would come along to fuck up her happiness.

"What does your gut say?" Evan asked.

Tears slid down her cheeks. "To trust you," she blurted. "You've acted like a dick in the past, but you've been good to me. I've stripped away most of my fears, but this one comes back over and over. I'm not an awful-looking person, but I keep wondering if I'm enough to keep you interested."

"I'm going to do something I never thought I'd do." Evan dropped to his knees right there in the foyer of their dorm. "Bliss McMahon, I love you. I don't have a ring, but you have my heart. One day, I'm going to marry you—if you'll have me. If you want time apart, you've got it, but you've also got my love."

"Evan." He'd proposed. Holy shit. What was he thinking?

"Do you love me?" he asked.

"I do." For the first time since they'd gotten together, she didn't doubt herself.

"Best thing I've ever heard." Evan tugged her onto his lap. "You're the best thing to ever happen to me."

"Just remember that while you're at the game." She hugged him tight.

"You know I will." He kissed her neck. "Seeing you in the crowd at the game and knowing you're the one I'm coming home to is the best feeling. You're the one I love, and being with you is the perfect reward."

"When are your folks getting here?" She left his lap and hauled him to his feet.

"About an hour." The light in his eyes flashed. "Plenty of time to go upstairs."

"Make love to me against the wall." She grasped his hand and hurried up to the dorm room.

"Weren't you going to wear a dress for supper with Mom and Dad?" Evan slipped the baby-doll dress off the hanger. "Put it on."

"Yeah?" She shrugged out of her coat then tossed both the coat and her purse onto the bed. She yanked the hem of her shirt over her head.

Evan eased up behind her. He smoothed his hands around her waist and helped her out of her jeans. "I've told you a thousand times that you're sexy, but I don't care. You are so hot, and I feel like a horny bastard." He kissed her shoulder then nipped her earlobe. "I want to be with you and inside you all the time."

"Yeah?" She slid the dress over her head. The skirt eased down her torso, but Evan kept her from being covered.

"Have I told you I love this dress on you? Perfect ease of access." Evan turned her around in his arms then pressed her to the wall. He stepped on her jeans, allowing her freedom from the denim. "I love this reward." He plucked a condom from the box. "Need you."

She draped her arms around his neck then hooked her leg around his waist. "I did wear a thong for you."

"Nice." Evan opened his fly and shoved his jeans to the floor. He didn't waste time with her thong and instead ripped the thin fabric.

Bliss kissed him and wiggled against him. Why let him take control all the time? She swallowed his moans and toyed with the hairs at the base of his neck. Slow, fast, however they made love, she wanted every moment.

He rolled the condom onto his dick then lined himself up with her opening. "Can't get enough of you." He pinned her between his torso and the wall. He gazed deep into her eyes and groaned.

Bliss met him thrust for thrust, loving the feel of him inside her. She squeezed him from within, trying to prolong the moment.

"Damn, that feels good." Evan licked her bottom lip. Hunger shone in his eyes, and he dug his fingers into her ass cheeks. "Mine." He crushed her against the wall with each push into her body. The animalistic tone of his voice turned her on even more. His breath heated her cheeks.

"I belong to you," she bit out. From the pit of her stomach and out to her limbs, she trembled. She couldn't catch her breath. The building orgasm overwhelmed her. Her skin sizzled. "Evan."

He said something she didn't understand and slammed into her. When he did, the orgasm crashed within her. She tensed all over then sagged in his arms.

"Fuck," he growled and filled her to the hilt. "Sweet Jesus." He pressed his face to her neck. His teeth raked her throat.

"I don't know how you do it." Bliss clung to Evan. One minute, she'd needed the space between them for clarity. The next, she didn't want him to go. It had to be something about him being her first love. Had to.

Evan pulled out of her and carried her to the bed. "Whatever I'm doing, I'm glad."

She flopped on the mattress and stared at the ceiling. "You said you've been in love before, right?'

"I have."

"How did you know?" She propped herself up on her elbows. "What was the *a-ha!* moment?"

Evan shrugged out of his jersey and hung the garment on the back of the desk chair. He glanced at himself in the mirror. "Well, my stomach hurt." He looked at her through the reflection and swiped his hair back into place. "No matter what I did, I didn't want to be away from her. It was almost like an obsession, but not."

"But not?" She crawled off the bed and smoothed her skirt into place. Underwear...she needed undergarments before going out into public. "What do you mean?"

Evan unbuttoned the collar of his dress shirt. "It was in high school. I never wanted to leave her side. Just touch her and kiss. To me, that was love. It was going to last forever. But it didn't. My grades slipped because I spent all my time with her. When we weren't together, she'd get pissed. Her parents hated me, and I did things out of character like sneaking out. I never had sex with her, but looking back, I know it wasn't really love."

She rummaged through the dresser drawer for her underwear. "How do you know this is different—you and me?"

Evan stood before her and buttoned his shirt. "For one thing, I could live without you if I wanted to, but I don't. I can stand to be apart from you, but a piece of me goes with you wherever you go. I trust you. Yes, I think about you when I'm at the ball field or in class, but it's not the crazy, obsessive can't-think-straight-until-I-see-you-again kind of thing. I know when I get back here, you'll be here or coming back here soon. Other guys look at you—and before you argue with me, they do—but I know you're coming home to me."

She clutched the panties in both hands. "You've got this maturity thing down pat."

"I've had to do some living." He gathered her in his arms. "You've been sheltered for a lot longer. I don't expect you to know exactly what you want, but I hope it's me."

*I know it is,* she wanted to say, but the words wouldn't come. She allowed him to kiss her. Once he pulled away, she stepped into her panties. Bliss donned her flats and a coat then followed him to the foyer.

She managed to get through dinner without embarrassing herself. No spills or sideways glances from Evan's parents. She'd held back the cringe when Evan announced he'd kind of proposed to her. Although his parents didn't glare, their smiles were tight. Bliss kept her mouth shut for the remainder of the night.

"We'll see you on Monday for spring break, correct?" Gene asked. He clapped Evan on the shoulder. "I've got plane tickets to Miami set aside for you."

"Me?" Evan asked. He snorted. "I don't know if I can. I've got games."

"Your sister was thinking about coming in. Maybe, she'd like it," Barbara suggested. "No problem."

Bliss folded her hands, lacing her fingers tightly together. She wasn't sure why, but the fact she hadn't been invited kind of pissed her off. His parents had been so cordial during Christmas. Maybe, their hesitance was a case of too much, too soon. Or they saw her immaturity.

"Give us a call, and we'll make time to get together." Gene waved to Bliss then hugged Evan. "Here's to a dozen more homeruns."

Barbara smiled at Bliss then snagged Evan in a hug, too. "Goodnight, son."

Once his parents were in their car and driving down the main street in front of the dorm, Evan sighed. "Well, that's a good sign."

"Oh yeah. A trip. You would've had fun." Bliss bit her tongue to keep from saying something mean.

"Huh? You mean Miami?" He shrugged. "They always go there about this time. My grandmother had property down there that my dad inherited. They get to hang out at the beach without the touristy crap."

"Oh."

"Oh is right. It's boring there. Yeah, it's on the beach, but it's my folks." He clasped her hand. "But I meant the visit went well."

"Are you crazy? Your mom hates me, and your dad just about choked when you brought up proposing. Makes me think they know something I don't—I'm not good enough for you." She let go of him and crept back. "They're probably right. Think about it. You've never met my family. I refuse to let you take me back home. Your friends make fun of me."

"Whoa." Evan burst out laughing. "Wow."

"What?" She hated him for making light of her situation.

"You took that in so many ways I never even thought of." He placed his finger over her lips. "Number one, the ticket thing was a test. If you didn't have a shit fit, Dad knew you were on the level. Remember the crazy, obsessed love thing? I'm sure you would love to go to Miami, but life won't end if we're apart. Number two, Mom likes all my girlfriends until they aren't just girlfriends any longer. This time she seemed to genuinely like my girlfriend. That's not her style, but I'm not questioning my good luck."

"Oh." She slid her hands underneath his coat and clutched the front of his shirt.

"As for going to your hometown, I don't want to. I heard you talk to your father one day when you thought Jessa and I were sleeping. I don't think I've ever heard someone so beat down in my life." He brushed his thumb across her bottom lip. "You're the woman I want. Whether my teammates like you or not, I don't care. My heart is in your hands." He smiled.

"Come upstairs. It's getting late, and I'm tired. I want to hold you."

She nodded and allowed him to walk her up to their dorm room. How lucky could one girl be? She had a great guy who loved her regardless of her flaws and was willing to give her what she needed. Yeah, she'd get the separation she wanted, but even without it, she knew down to her soul that she loved and trusted Evan Phillips. He hadn't left yet, but once he came home, she'd show him just how much she loved him.

# Chapter Fourteen

Sunday evening, Bliss stared at the telephone. The first quarter of the year had come and gone with no fanfare from her mother or father. She'd expected never to hear from her mother, but she hadn't even gotten a phone call from her father. Though Jan hated her, her dad had always called her.

She dug through her address book for the last phone number she'd been given for her mother. Bliss' hand trembled as she dialed the digits. Since she'd been in college, she'd talked to her mother exactly once. Would her mother even answer?

After three rings, someone picked up on the other end. "Hello?"

"Hi, this is Bliss McMahon. My mother told me I could contact her at this number. Is Doreen McMahon there?" Bliss gripped the telephone.

"Doreen? Just a moment." The other end of the line snapped and crackled then conversation could be heard but nothing made out. After a moment, the scratching sound stopped.

"Hello? Bliss?"

Bliss blew out a long breath. "Mom?"

"Hi, baby. I haven't heard from you in so long," Doreen said. "Did you get the money I sent for Christmas?"

"Money? Where did you send it?" She couldn't remember the last time her mother sent a Christmas card, let alone money.

"To the house. It's got your name on it."

"I haven't been home."

"Oh? Why not? Is that nasty Jan keeping you out?"

"It's a lot of stuff." Bliss blinked back tears. Her mother actually sounded as if she cared.

"Then tell me. I might not be there, but I'm still your mother." The other end of the line went silent for a long moment. "Bliss, honey, I never got the chance to tell you I'm sorry. I know this is awful timing, and I don't sound like I mean it, but I do. I never should've run off to California without taking you along."

"Mom, I wouldn't have fit in out there. I'm too…boring." She brushed the tears away. "I like being here in Kenton."

"I forgot. You're a junior in college. Where has the time gone?" Doreen laughed then her voice cracked. "I've missed so much."

"I passed my portfolio review and signed up for my assignment for student teaching next year. I'm almost done."

"I'm proud of you."

"I've got a boyfriend, too." Well, she thought she did. After pushing him away, she'd be lucky if he truly wanted her back.

"Good. You deserve to be happy. When I get to Ohio again, I'm coming to see you."

Bliss exchanged addresses with her mother and passed along her phone number. "I love you, Mom." This time, Bliss' voice cracked. "I wish you were here."

"I wish I was, too. Love you, baby." Her mother hung up, leaving Bliss in silence. More tears streamed down Bliss' cheeks. Maybe it was lip service, but they'd made a breakthrough. She believed her mother. Yes, Doreen wasn't going to be in Bliss' life full-time, but the assumed hatred and regret wasn't there.

She blew out another long breath. According to her calendar, her father's birthday was in less than two days. She had time to call him and privacy to do so.

Fuck it. Time to put her upset aside and call her father. She dialed the number and waited for someone to pick up.

"Hello?"

Bliss measured her breaths. Jan. "Hi, Jan. It's Bliss."

"Who?" Jan snapped. She knew damn well who was on the other end of the line.

"Bliss. I'd like to talk to Dad."

"I'm sorry, we don't want any. Thank you," Jan said. In the background, Bliss heard her father ask who was on the line.

"Daddy, it's me," Bliss shouted.

"Look, you little brat," Jan growled. "You're the most ungrateful bitch. You only call when you want something. We are not your personal bank. Got it? Your father has better things to do than talk to his waste of a child."

"How's Avery?" Bliss asked, despite her voice breaking and tears streaming down her cheeks.

"She's fine. She's taking private lessons on the trumpet so she can compete in the local beauty pageant."

"That's great. Can I talk to Dad? Please?"

"I said no." Jan's end of the line clicked as Bliss' father picked up.

"Jan, give me a moment with my daughter," he said. "Go on."

"You have one daughter. That's enough," Jan snapped, but she clicked off the line.

Bliss clapped her hand across her mouth to stifle the cries. God damn it. What had she ever done to Jan to make her so bitter?

"Hi, Bliss. You didn't come home for Christmas. No call, no arrival. I'd say I was worried, but Jan said you'd told her you weren't planning on coming home. Is that true?"

"I didn't call, but I wasn't going to go home. I'm not welcome there. Jan told me the next time I showed up, she'd throw me out. I didn't want to cause trouble, so I went home with my boyfriend." She forced herself to breathe slowly. "He's a good man, Dad. You'd like him."

"I bet I would." Her dad sighed. "Bliss, honey, I'm sorry. The situation here has been tense, but I never want you to think you're not welcome at the house. You're my daughter just as much as Avery."

"Thanks, Daddy." She choked back another cry. "I didn't think you wanted me home."

"I do. We'll have to work around Jan, but I do. I've got some gifts here for you and an envelope from your mother. When I tried to call you, that nasty roommate of yours must not have passed along the messages."

"I got kicked out of my room. It's a long story, Dad, but I didn't do anything wrong. It was a mess." She blotted her face with tissues. "I miss you, Dad."

"I miss you, too, honey. I'll get that envelope from your mother sent up there tomorrow. Let me know it arrives, okay?"

"Thanks, Dad. Happy birthday. I made a drawing for you and passed my portfolio review. I'll be student teaching in the fall."

"Wonderful and thank you. The best present is knowing you're safe and happy. I'm proud of you, Bliss." He grunted. "I've got to go. Jan has some sort of disaster happening. I love you, baby."

"Love you, too, Dad. Goodnight." She placed the phone back into the cradle and leaned against the wall. Life wasn't perfect, but the things she'd thought were true weren't. She switched off the light and flopped back on the bed. Once Evan got back, she'd sort out that part of her life in order to heal and move forward—hopefully, with him.

\* \* \* \*

Evan sat on the bus after the game. His head ached. Although he'd hit three homeruns and helped win the first game of the double-header, he'd taken a baseball to the side of his head. The helmet had helped dissipate some of the impact, but not all. He'd made it to first base without issue, but when the shortstop had fielded the line-drive, his throw had gone wild and connected with Evan's head.

The doctor had cleared him of any concussion symptoms, but warned he'd have a nasty headache. The doctor wasn't wrong.

Evan closed his eyes and ignored the conversation around him. A win and a loss meant the team wasn't as chatty as with a double win. Thank God. He needed the silence. Soon, they'd be on the road and home.

"There you are." The seat beside him moved, and Jessa's perfume wrapped around him.

The dull ache in his head increased. "Your perfume is thick."

"I need to be able to smell it." She scooted down in the seat and dug her knees into the back of the seat in front of her. "How's your head?"

"Fine." Not really, but he didn't want to talk to her. "Isn't Dalton on the bus? He's your new man, right? Go sit with him."

"We're taking a break." She slid her arm around his and rested her head on his shoulder. "I hear you and Bliss are taking a break, too."

"If you mean me going to the game and her staying behind because she has work for her student teaching class, then yes, we're taking a break." He yanked his hand from hers. "Please go. I'm not in the mood to deal with you."

"I know you." She plunked her palm on his thigh. "We're good together." She walked her fingers up his leg to his crotch and stroked him through the fabric of his jeans. "Feel that? I make you happy, and I'm right here with you."

"No." Evan grabbed her hand and placed it back on her lap. "Stop."

"Stop?" she snapped. "Please. I'm the best you're going to get."

"I doubt that." He gritted his teeth. Listening to her increased the ache behind his eyes. Fuck. Between her perfume and her presence, he needed her to go away.

"You love my hand jobs." She massaged him more, mashing his dick under his zipper.

He removed her hand a second time. "Don't want one."

"Why? You're all tense."

"I'm not interested," he bit out. "Go."

She growled and folded her arms. "You really like Bliss, don't you?"

"I do." No point in denying the truth.

"I don't get it. You could have any girl on campus — me, if you asked — but you chose her. She's not even pretty. She's...gag."

"Enough." Evan opened his eyes and glared at her.

"She makes cattle look thin." Jessa twirled a lock of her hair around her finger. "She's most likely to go through life alone."

"Jessa. Haven't you said enough? God, you're the bitterest person I know." He put his arm between them. "I've got a headache, and I don't feel like talking. Go away."

"Please. You're tired of hearing the truth." She grasped his forearm. "She's a heifer, and that's being mean to the cows. Dump her, and come home to me."

"Enough." Evan put both hands in the air to block her. "I used to think you were a sweet, tender-hearted girl who made me happy. I knew you weren't the one I'd settle down with, but we were good in bed. Now, I've seen your true colors. I'm glad I moved on. I'm happier with you out of my life."

Jessa stood and blocked the aisle. "I should've known. You're a loser. You'll find out when you go pro. She's only with you as a ticket to the better life. When you get there and fall flat on your face, she'll be gone. I know the truth. You won't amount to anything. You suck, and your batting average is only high because you're getting a blowjob."

"Aren't you positive?"

"I know the truth." She lowered her voice to a growl. "When she fucks you over, don't you dare come crying to me. I don't give a shit any longer." She flounced down the aisle toward the back of the bus.

*Good riddance.* Evan folded his hands on his belly and closed his eyes. The aspirin had started to work, but not much.

"Mind if I sit here?" Coach asked. "I'd like to keep an eye on you. That blow to your noggin was rough."

"No kidding." Evan opened his eyes and moved over. "It still hurts, but it's not awful."

"You're stoic." Coach settled next to him on the seat. "You had a good game, despite the conk on the head. I'm proud of you." He stretched his legs and gripped his ball cap. His salt-and-pepper hair stuck fast to his head, and the crinkles around his eyes deepened.

Evan nodded slightly. The vote of approval from Coach resonated in Evan's head. He'd thought he'd played well, but he liked hearing the words out loud.

"On a sour note, I saw Jessa annoying you." Coach replaced his hat on his head. "Please tell me you're not together again."

"Nope. Very much done." He brushed his hands on his pant legs. So ready to move on and head home to Bliss. He wanted to make up for their time apart.

"Good on the Jessa thing. She's been a boil on my ass since she signed up to do the stats." Coach shook his head. "I noticed your batting average and overall outlook improved once you two parted ways. She's a distraction."

The lights dowsed on the bus, and the vehicle moved forward.

"She wasn't good for me, no. She's moved on to Dalton Greene." He stared out the window at the lights glittering in the parking lot. Something his ex had said stuck in his brain. "Jessa seemed to think I was going to make the pros—until we split. Then she swore I couldn't play for shit. True?"

Coach sighed. "If you decide to go into the majors, you'll lag in the minors for a while. You might get called up late season when other players get hurt, but you're not material for the pros, no. Now, I say this not because I think you're a bad player. Your heart is in the game, but you don't have the conviction to get into the majors. That's not a bad thing. I'd rather have players who want to play for the love of the game than guys who just want to move to the next level. Your mind is on the game here. Some of my other players are long gone before they even leave college."

Evan allowed himself a moment to mull over what Coach had said. Honestly, he'd always sort of figured he wasn't cut out for the pros. He wanted to teach and help others reach their dreams. The idea of getting hurt and potentially ruining his career before he even started also filled his mind. He'd been hurt today and didn't want to wreck his head with another injury.

"That's what I needed to know. Thanks." Evan settled in his seat. His mind eased. "I'm good."

"Why? Were you thinking about the majors? Last I knew, you were going to finish your education degree and teach."

"My plan is to have a degree, yes. If college-level ball is my limit, I'm perfectly happy with where I'm at. I surpassed my expectations, and now, it's time to move on to the next chapter of my life. I'm good with being an amateur. I'd rather use my skills on the field to teach kids like me and help them chase their dreams. Maybe, I'll become a coach wherever I end up teaching." He could actually see himself working with a varsity team. Teaching during the day, coaching in the afternoon and going home to Bliss at night. Wouldn't life be great?

"You'd be a good coach. You've got compassion and don't put up with bullshit, but you know how to motivate."

"Cool." Evan rested his head against the chilly window glass. The brisk temperature helped ease his headache a bit more.

"Speaking of cool, word on the street is that you're seeing someone from the School of Art. Missy?"

Evan's ears perked. He glanced in Coach's direction. "Bliss. She came to the Christmas party and usually comes to the home games." He could've sworn he'd introduced her to Coach, but now, he wasn't so sure.

"Is she brunette? I think I remember her." Coach nodded and chuckled. "Anyway, hold on to her. She's a keeper."

Evan frowned. "You know her?" Something didn't make sense. "Did I introduce you two?"

"No, but I know her. I never said anything because I didn't want to stir the pot if you had issues with her, but she babysat for us last year and over the summer. Darcy always called her Missy. Kate and I loved having her watch Darcy because she was always on time and left the house cleaner than when she showed up. She's good with kids, and even if her parents are shits, she's got a good head on her shoulders."

"She does." Evan smiled to himself. He'd poured his heart out to Bliss. He loved her and trusted his gut. Yes, she'd wanted to take a break, but he knew what he needed to do next.

## Chapter Fifteen

Four hours later, the bus stopped at the student lot next to the recreational center. Evan picked up his bag and his gear bag then made his way to the car. He glanced at the clock. Damn. Past midnight. Thank God, he didn't have a Monday morning class and his latest philosophy paper had been turned in before he'd left for the weekend. He drove across campus to the dorm. Thankfully, a parking spot in front of the building was open. He pulled into the spot and stopped. Down to his bones, tiredness overwhelmed him. He didn't need the gear bag, so he left that in the trunk and only grabbed his overnight bag.

Something his father had said came to mind. *You've got to do what your gut tells you to do.*

What did his gut tell him? To follow his heart to Bliss? Or to retract his statement about wanting to marry her? He locked his car and trudged up the four flights of stairs to his room.

Part of him wasn't thrilled about her attitude shift. How could she do this to him? Did she really want to be apart or was this just fear? The rest of him wasn't ready to walk away.

He loved her and understood her uneasiness. They'd jumped headlong into a relationship, and she hadn't had many relationships before. He hoped she wasn't second-guessing them getting together. As far as he was concerned, he'd found the love of his life.

He stuffed the key into the knob then opened the door and hurried inside before he flooded the room with light. After a moment, his eyes adjusted to the scant light coming in from the window. He dropped his bag on the floor, his keys on the desk and kicked out of his shoes. Laying down sounded so good—especially with Bliss. They'd sort out the issues between them in the morning.

He stripped out of his clothes and down to his boxer shorts then climbed into bed with her. He pressed his belly to her back and draped his arm around her. Being with her settled him.

Bliss wrapped her hand around his. "You're home."

"I am." He kissed the back of her neck. "Couldn't wait to get back here to you. I missed you."

She rolled over and faced him. In the dim light, her eyes shimmered. "I missed you, too." She rested her forehead against his. "So much."

"Did you?" His heart leapt. Maybe, they had a chance after all.

"I'm sorry I didn't trust you and acted immature." She slid her palm over his ass and sighed. "I was wrong."

"About what?" The sleep faded. He focused on her and where the conversation was heading.

"Being apart. Having a cool-down period." She shrugged. "It sounded good on paper, but in reality, it sucked. I finally got what you meant by the neurotic need to be together and the bone-deep desire. I can live without you, but I don't want to."

"We're on the same wavelength." Evan kissed the tip of her nose. "Your idea to spend some time apart was good. It gave me time to think. Jessa was there." He draped his arm around her waist and eased his fingers beneath the hem of her sleep shirt.

"Oh." Her hand stilled. "How was she?"

"Her normal self. That's just it. I saw all of her true colors—not that I didn't know what they were to begin with. She got me thinking, too. I've got a lot of big decisions in my near future. I don't want to mess them up." He trailed his fingers up and down her spine. "Answer a question for me. If I wasn't a ballplayer, would you still love me and want to be with me?"

"Yes, I would. You're kind, handsome, caring, sweet and patient beyond belief. You've got flaws, sure, but who doesn't? Any woman would be crazy not to want to be with you. Why?"

She hadn't hesitated, despite being tired, and she'd been honest. Evan tamped down his excitement. He needed to answer her question first. "When we graduate, my baseball career will be over. I'm not going out for the majors because I want to teach. I'm fully decided on teaching. Coach even told me I don't have the conviction to play in the pros."

"You told me that was your plan, but your coach…he's half-right and half-wrong." She moved her hand from his butt to his chest over his heart. "You have the conviction, but it's not what your heart desires."

She understood him so well. Evan inched closer to her, pressing his groin to hers. "You're right. I want to coach and use my degree." He rolled onto his back and pulled her onto his lap. Her hair shimmered in the moonlight.

Bliss grasped his hands. "As long as you're happy, coaching and teaching is what you should do. I can't see myself doing anything other than art."

"You're okay with my plans?" He needed to know, beyond a shadow of a doubt, she believed in him and would be his partner.

"Absolutely."

God, he loved her. "Jessa wasn't okay with how I'd planned out my future. She said it was all wrong. Then again, she seemed to think hooking up with me was going to bring her celebrity and money. I needed to be sure you weren't like her."

"I'm not. Fame is the last thing I want." She snorted. "That's Jessa. She's not happy unless she's the center of attention." Bliss stretched out on top of him and rested her chin on her folded hands. "It's funny that you mentioned her. She was one of the most negative forces in my life. I can't be happy with who I am until some of those forces are gone. So, I talked to both my mother and father tonight."

That was a curveball he hadn't seen coming. "You haven't spoken to your mom in years. I'm proud of you." Evan petted her hair. "Want to talk about it?"

"The calls were and weren't what I expected. Mom seemed genuinely happy to hear from me. She said she sent me a Christmas present. First one in a dozen years. Presents are good, but she actually said she was proud of me. She hasn't been that…ever." Bliss smiled, but the corner of her mouth twitched as if she couldn't quite hold the expression.

"Time gives people the chance to think through decisions." He sounded like a greeting card, but who cared? She needed him to be a rock, and damn it, he'd be that rock.

"We'll see when the envelope arrives." Bliss shrugged. A tear splashed onto his chest. "When I called Dad, Jan answered. She called me the customary names and yelled. But for the first time since I left for college, Dad actually intervened. Was it a miracle? I'm not sure, but he tried. He was hurt I hadn't come home for Christmas and said we'd work around Jan. Will it all work out? I don't know, but he made the effort and allowed me to move forward. That gigantic weight is gone. They're flawed, but they are my parents, and I don't have to answer to them all the time."

"You stood up for yourself. I'm proud of you. You are amazing." Evan wiped the tears from her cheeks. "I've always got your back. Always."

"Thanks." She sighed and tangled her legs with his. "I saw the game on television. The campus channel carried it. You were great. How's your head?" She slid her fingers through his hair on the side opposite the lump. "The hit didn't look so good, but that throw to first from the outfield to get the runner out in the ninth was awesome."

"My head is still attached so I'm good."

Bliss smiled again, and it reached her eyes. "You're silly, but I'm glad you're back. I love you."

She'd grown so much just in the days they'd been apart and even more in the few months they'd been together. "I love you, too, babe, which is why I'm sure I want to marry you." No worries, no regrets. He reached for the drawer to the desk and fumbled for the velvet pouch. He'd hidden his class ring in the desk after they'd returned from Christmas break. Until he got her a proper engagement ring, the thick class ring would have to do. "Bliss McMahon, will you marry me?" He held up the ring. "I know this isn't a diamond, but it's from the heart. You're the one I love and the one I want for the rest of my life."

"Evan." She touched the ring. "I... Wow."

"Is that a yes? Or a maybe?" He eased the thick band of metal onto her middle finger. "Something?"

"It's a yes. Totally yes." She admired the ring then leaned over and kissed him. "It's time for us to get out of the dorms."

"And find an apartment of our own." Evan wound his arms around her again. Her sweetness poured all over him with each kiss.

Bliss broke the connection then climbed off his lap long enough to pluck a condom from the box on the desk. She tore open the packet.

"Yes." Evan shrugged out of his boxer shorts then reached for her. "Come here."

She grinned as she sheathed him. Bliss' touch lingered on his balls. She caressed him, kicking his need for her up a few notches. He groaned. She knew how to satisfy him better than anyone. He rocked his hips, thrusting into her hand and rubbing on her.

"You'll come before I get a chance to ride." She whipped her sleep shirt up over her head, leaving her in nothing but her panties.

"You're teasing me, beautiful."

"I know." She shoved her panties down her hips then stepped out of the garment and climbed back onto his lap. She lined up his cock with her pussy. "It's fun to tease you."

"Bad girl." He grasped her waist, plunging her onto his cock. "God. I needed this and you."

Bliss leaned over him and clasped his hands. The move put her breasts right within his reach. Evan sucked her nipple into his mouth. He bit then licked the tight bundle of nerves in time with his thrusts.

"Wow," she murmured.

The ring rubbed against his knuckle as she squeezed his hands tight. He didn't care. He'd take whatever pain and pleasure she'd give him as long as they were together. One day, he'd be bare inside her. They'd be married. Another groan ripped from his throat.

He pulled away from her and panted. Heat flowed through his body. His cock throbbed. Each time he plunged into her cunt, she clamped down on him. Oh, shit. He wasn't going to last.

"Evan," she bit out. Bliss rolled her hips, changing the angle of his thrusts slightly and pushing him much closer to orgasm.

"Fuck." Evan tucked her to his chest then rolled and pinned her beneath him. Having her on top was heaven, but the animalistic desire to claim her took over. He planted his knees on the bed. Body and soul, he belonged to her. He pushed within her until the tension in his body uncoiled. His restraint broke, and he gritted his teeth.

"Evan," she said a second time. Bliss curled her legs around his waist. She trembled and whimpered.

When he breathed out, the orgasm overtook him. Evan braced himself on his knees and hands and rested his forehead against hers. "I'll never get enough."

She closed her eyes and nodded.

Evan stayed inside her but didn't speak. He basked in the moment. The world could've come crashing down around them, but he wouldn't have cared. He'd scored the biggest run of his life when he'd met her.

"Never letting you go," Evan whispered.

"I'm not letting you go, either." Bliss snuggled beneath him. "Love you."

"Love you, too." He feathered kisses all over her lips, cheeks and chin. He could live without her but didn't want to. She was the one he'd been looking for all along. The best stolen base ever.

After he ditched the used condom and crawled back into bed with her, Evan stared at the ceiling and chuckled. A fiancée. He'd never have imagined six months ago that he'd be engaged to the woman of his dreams. He knew what he wanted next. Their own apartment. Once they were done with the school year, they'd get a place off campus that was all theirs.

"What are you thinking about?" Bliss draped her arm across his bare chest. The thick class ring glittered on the middle finger of her left hand. He owned her heart, and she owned his. He was the luckiest man alive.

He sighed. "I'm dog tired, but my brain won't shut off."

"About what?"

"All the planning we'll have to do in addition to finishing college." The idea of picking out invitations and choosing colors bored him to tears, but he'd do whatever she wanted. They had plenty of time.

"I say we run off to Vegas. Keep it simple. Plus, the honeymoon is part of the package. Once the deed is done, we go upstairs for the rest of the festivities." She giggled and closed her hand over his heart. "Know what I mean?"

"I do, and I'm onboard with your idea." He kissed the top of her head. "What about late January?" All sorts of ideas popped into his brain. If they wanted to leave the hotel room, they could, but if not, everything was a phone call away. What a great way to spend the first few nights of marriage. "Cool enough to walk the strip if we want to or cold enough to stay in and keep each other warm."

"January is good. No, it's perfect." Bliss ensnared him in her embrace. "Is this what you had in mind when you started college? Hooking up a ton of times only to find your best friend? Be honest."

"I saw myself having a cat, too."

"We can get one. We'd have to get an apartment, first."

"That can be arranged. Coach mentioned something about bringing me on as an assistant coach. If you can balance a job while we're in our last year, we should be okay." Okay? They'd be golden. Evan chuckled. "Three years ago, I thought by this time I'd be out of college and playing ball professionally. I'd have the hottest girl and be making a shitload of money. Looking back, I see where it would've been cool, but not me. Pro baseball is great, and I'm glad there are guys who can. I'm good. I've got less than a year left until I can teach others to play. The woman of my dreams turned out to be better than I could've expected, and I'm marrying her. I'm happy—and yeah, we should get a cat."

"I agree. When I first met you, I wished you weren't having sex on the bed below me, but it got us together." Bliss tucked in closer to him. "I'm glad you went for extra bases and stole home."

"Best move I ever made." Life would never be boring with Bliss. She lit up the room and his existence. Because of her, he chased his dreams with abandon. Everything happened for a reason, and now that he had her, he wouldn't change a thing.

# *Epilogue*

*Ten Years Later…*

Evan raked his fingers through his hair then replaced his ball cap. "One more round, guys." He pointed to the running track. "It's not all about standing in the outfield and watching the daisies grow. The faster you get around the track, the more time we've got for your reward for winning the division title."

He folded his arms. His life had changed so much in the last ten years. After hooking up with Bliss, he finished his college career, and within months had a teaching position near his hometown of Oleana. He'd married Bliss in Vegas the January before graduation, just as she'd suggested. They didn't have a ton of money, but with his job teaching middle school physical education and coaching on the side, they made a good living. Bliss taught private art lessons and substitute taught at the high school.

"Hey, there's Daddy." Bliss strolled up to Evan. She bounced their son, Logan, on her hip.

"Came to see the excitement?" Evan asked. He scooped Logan away from Bliss. "You'll be bigger than Mom in a few years." He ruffled Logan's hair. He'd already begun working with the two-year-old to hit a baseball and to catch.

"Couldn't miss it." Bliss chuckled. "You've got your dream."

"I do." Evan draped one arm around her shoulders. He did have everything he wanted. Teaching, coaching, a family… The mistake he'd thought he'd made by dating the wrong girl had turned out to be the stepping stone he needed to find the right path for his life.

The players gathered around Evan, Logan and Bliss. Some of them waved to Bliss, while others said hi.

"It took us three years and a few personnel changes to get to the playoffs, but we did it. I'm proud of you guys and all the hard work you've put in. Now, some of you are going to college on scholarships to play ball. I could give you the standard speech about knowing what you're getting into before getting your hopes up. I know because I've been in your shoes. Instead, I've got one of my friends and Hawks player,

Xavier Nelson. He started out right where you all did and made it into the majors." Evan stepped aside. "Xave?"

Decked out in his uniform and cleats, Xavier strode up to the group. He gripped the bat he'd rested on his shoulder. "First things first. This guy you call a coach is... You couldn't ask for a better coach."

Evan glanced over at the players. A couple rolled their eyes while a few of them stared at Xavier. He shook his head. Trust Xavier to make a big deal.

"When I was back in college, Coach, here, told me to see my goals through. I admired his honesty. While most of the guys we played with on the team were dead set on becoming the next homerun derby king, Coach Phillips planned on coming back to his roots. Because of his decision, the scouts looked at me." He grinned. "They did, but I'm glad. Having a coach at this level who encourages you and gets you wanting to go for more is one of the biggest stepping stones for getting to the majors."

The players erupted in applause. Evan shook his head again. "Better you than some of the others."

"Ah, yes." Xavier winked. He turned his attention back to the players. "Besides, Coach Phillips got the girl. That's pretty rad, too."

"Rad?" one of the players asked. "No one says rad anymore."

The tips of Xavier's ears turned red.

"Some of us do," Evan replied. "I say it all the time. Ask Mrs. Phillips. Anyway, as your reward, Xavier and I are going to divvy the team up. He gets half and I get half for a totally for-fun game. Sound good?"

The group cheered. Evan handed Logan back to Bliss. "Promise me you'll have the heating pad and the ice ready when I blow out my knee again."

She laughed at him then kissed his cheek. "You're old, but not that old, handsome." She winked at him. "Remember, stealing home got you everything you wanted. Can't hurt to try that again."

He kissed her on the lips then chuckled as she made her way over to the bleachers. He *had* gotten everything he wanted when he'd gone for the extra bases. Stealing home was a great idea all the way.

# About the Author

Wendi Zwaduk is a multi-published, award-winning author of more than one-hundred short stories and novels. She's been writing since 2008 and published since 2009. Her stories range from the contemporary and paranormal to BDSM and LGBTQ themes. No matter what the length, her works are always hot, but with a lot of heart. She enjoys giving her characters a second chance at love, no matter what the form. She's been the runner up in the Kink Category at Love Romances Café as well as nominated at the LRC for best contemporary, best ménage and best anthology. Her books have made it to the bestseller lists on Amazon.com and the former AllRomance Ebooks. She also writes under the name of Megan Slayer.

When she's not writing, she spends time with her husband and son as well as three dogs and three cats. She enjoys art, music and racing, but football is her sport of choice. Find out more about Wendi at: https://www.wendizwaduk.comhttp://www.wendizwaduk.com/ or on her blog: https://wendizwaduk.wordpress.com/

Find her on Facebook, Twitter, Instagram, Bookbub, Goodreads and Amazon.

# Books by Megan Slayer/Wendi Zwaduk

## Track Domination Series
Hot Laps
Running Hot
Switching Gears
Finding Grip
Making a Mark

## Club Desire Series
Tide Desire
Bases Loaded
All on the Field
Desiring the Leading Man
Needing Desire
Taking Desire
Blue Satin

## Complicated Series
Complicated
Off Camera
Stealing Home

# *Also Available in the* Complicated *Series*

## *Complicated by Megan Slayer*
**Complicated Series, Book One**

*Finding the love of your life is hard, especially when you're young and in the movies.*

Jonathan Reynolds came to Cleveland, Ohio to break into the movies. He might not have the most orthodox methods, but he's got the drive. He wants to be a star and shed his small town image. He's no kid, although at twenty-one, he's not very experienced. He's happy with only having a few lines during a crowd scene—until he meets Sean Banks. Maybe it's time for this virgin to come of age.

Sean Banks has been there, done that—on everything. The former child star grew up in the glare of the spotlight and beat his addiction to drugs and alcohol. But at twenty-four, he's considered all washed up. He knows the role in this high budget action picture will catapult him back into the spotlight. He's not ready to open his heart again, until he sees Jonathan. The young man captivates him. Can the jaded former star and the up-and-coming actor find common ground and passion between the sheets? Or will their love be relegated to the silver screen?

## *Off Camera by Megan Slayer*
**Complicated Series, Book Two**

*Navigating college is hard, but not as hard as learning to love and trust.*

Kade Evans knew what he wanted to do with his life—write scripts for Hollywood. He's poured his heart into his work and learning the tricks of the trade, but being only twenty-one he knows he needs experience. How's a guy supposed to get experience when he's shy and quiet? The answer might be closer and more forceful than he thinks.

Tony Victor's goal in life is to make movies. He won't quit until he's working on the next blockbuster. First, he's got to get through college and get the handsome guy from script writing class to notice him. Tony's never had trouble getting attention, but something about Kade calls to him. Tony's head says go slow, but his heart is ready to take things to the next level.

Will these two find common ground or will the simmering passion between them fall apart when their secrets are revealed?

*Warning: When the camera comes on, these sexy college guys deliver sizzling, unscripted – x-rated – pleasure.*

AVON LAKE PUBLIC LIBRARY
32649 ELECTRIC BOULEVARD
AVON LAKE, OHIO 44012

27939091R00129

Made in the USA
Columbia, SC
02 October 2018